Shoot-Out at
Sugar Creek

Also by Mickey Spillane and Max Allan Collins

The Legend of Caleb York

The Big Showdown

The Bloody Spur

Last Stage to Hell Junction

Hot Lead, Cold Justice

Masquerade for Murder

Murder, My Love

Killing Town

The Will to Kill

A Long Time Dead

Murder Never Knocks

Kill Me, Darling

King of the Weeds

Complex 90

Lady, Go Die!

The Consummata

Kiss Her Goodbye

The Big Bang

The Goliath Bone

Dead Street

MICKEY SPILLANE
AND
MAX ALLAN COLLINS

Shoot-Out at Sugar Creek

KENSINGTON
PUBLISHING CORP.

www.kensingtonbooks.com

KENSINGTON BOOKS are published by

Kensington Publishing Corp.
119 West 40th Street
New York, NY 10018

All Kensington titles, imprints, and distributed lines are available at special quantity discounts for bulk purchases for sales promotion, premiums, fund-raising, educational, or institutional use. Special book excerpts or customized printings can also be created to fit specific needs. For details, write or phone the office of the Kensington Special Sales Manager: Attn. Special Sales Department. Kensington Publishing Corp, 119 West 40th Street, New York, NY 10018. Phone: 1-800-221-2647.

The K logo is a trademark of Kensington Publishing Corp.

Library of Congress Control Number: 2020952336

ISBN-13: 978-1-4967-3012-1
ISBN-10: 1-4967-3012-7
First Kensington Hardcover Edition: May 2021

ISBN-13: 978-1-4967-3013-8 (ebook)
ISBN-10: 1-4967-3013-5 (ebook)

10 9 8 7 6 5 4 3 2 1

Printed in the United States of America

For Stuart Rosebrook,
my True Western pal
who also rides the Iowa range

"They deal in life and sudden death
and primitive struggle,
and with the basic emotions—love, hate,
and anger—thrown in."
—John Wayne, on Westerns

Spillane and Wayne

I remember vividly the lovely warm, sunny South Carolina afternoon when, as we sat sipping Miller beer in his outdoor tiki bar, Mickey Spillane told me that his famous private eye, Mike Hammer, was designed to be a modern-day equivalent of the mythic Western hero.

"He wears the black hat," he said, "but he does the right thing."

Like most of the great Western heroes of fiction and film, Hammer used the methods of the villains he'd pursued to get his man . . . and sometimes woman.

This led Mickey to say on that afternoon, somewhat surprisingly, "I wrote a Western once, you know."

Well, I didn't know.

He went on to tell me about a screenplay, "The Saga of Calli York," that he'd written for his old friend John Wayne. He and Wayne had been thick in Mickey's early 1950s heyday, and the Mick had even starred in a circus mystery the Duke produced, *Ring of Fear* (1954). You can find it on DVD—color and Cinema-

Scope, with Mickey playing himself but channeling Mike Hammer.

If you're a Spillane fan, you may know that Wayne gave Mickey a white Jaguar convertible by way of payment for Mike Hammer's papa rewriting the script of that troubled film. Less than a decade later, Mickey would star in the Hammer movie *The Girl Hunters*, produced by longtime Wayne associate Robert Fellows. Of course, Mickey's most famous acting role was as a pitchman for Miller Lite, sporting a porkpie hat and trenchcoat, a doll (well, *The* Doll) on his arm. That series of commercials only lasted eighteen years.

"You wanna see it?" Mickey asked, getting back to the Western movie script he'd announced having written.

Of course I did. He sent it home with me (he once called me his "human wastebasket").

Shortly before his death in 2006, Mickey asked me to complete the final Mike Hammer, then in progress (*The Goliath Bone*), if need be. I, of course, said yes. And then (without telling me) he instructed his wife, Jane, to turn over all of the rest of his unpublished materials to me. I would know what to do, he said.

That has led to thirteen Mike Hammer books—all expanded from unfinished Spillane manuscripts or outlines—and two non-Hammer novels. More are on the way—Mickey's files were extensive, to say the least. But only when I mentioned to my editor at Kensington—where, in addition to mysteries, Westerns are a specialty—that I had an unproduced screenplay written by Spillane for Wayne, well . . .

Now we have arrived at the sixth Caleb York novel ("Calli" is a nickname I dropped), developed from various drafts of that script. I hope Mickey would be pleased.

I think he would. I like to think both he and the Duke would get a kick out of them.

But the readers—his "customers," as Mickey put it—are what counts. I hope you will be a satisfied one, reading this new Caleb York yarn.

Max Allan Collins

CHAPTER ONE

In the flickering yellow light of a brass oil lamp, Caleb York, seated at his big beat-up wooden desk, filed through wanted posters like a card player checking the deadwood discards for an ace that had eluded him.

Closing in on forty, but not too fast, York was a big man yet lean, his jaw firm, his reddish brown hair gray at the temples. His pleasant features softened their raw-boned, clean-shaven setting, his eyes the color of well-worn denim and fixed in an all but permanent squint.

His gray shirt with pearl buttons and black string tie, and the black cotton pants tucked in hand-tooled black boots, said city—as did the black frock coat hung on a nearby wall peg, a calvary-pinched black hat on another peg next to it. But the gun belt with Colt Single Action Army .44—coiled on his desk like a rattler waiting to be roused—said something else.

He was the county sheriff—and de facto marshal—of Trinidad, New Mexico (population three hundred or so but growing), alone in a plank-floored jailhouse office whose two barred street windows were letting in only darkness. The wood-burning stove was unlit—this was April, the worst winter in anybody's memory mercifully over, but the smell of spring flowers on the prairies had been supplanted by the stench of death.

Here in town, at least, the bouquet of horse manure and the whiff of beans cooking across the way in the modest barrio represented the normal scent of spring in the Southwest. Not that anything much was normal about the aftermath of what folks were calling the Big Die-Up.

The snow had begun last November, a seeming relief after the Hades-like heat of a dry summer, worse the farther north you went, Montana, Wyoming, the Black Hills. By early January, plateaus were painted a crystalline pearl, dry river bottoms buried beneath drifting white. Cattle starved to death by the thousands, owners caught flat-footed without enough hay stored for such a disaster. New Mexico hadn't been hit quite as hard, but hard enough. The spring roundup—hence, "die-up"—would not happen at all, which meant hardship for ranchers in the area, in particular Willa Cullen and her Bar-O.

Willa was of a special concern to York, whose relationship with the willful young woman—who had inherited the biggest ranch in these parts from an otherwise childless father—had, over the near year York had been here, gone from cool to warm to cold to (more recently) hot, pleasantly so.

When he'd ridden into Trinidad, he'd been a nameless nobody, just passing through, on a westbound journey on which he had benefited from a rumor that Caleb York—celebrated Wells Fargo detective notorious for *not* bringing them back alive—had been shot down like a dog. He'd decided to leave it that way, at least until he got to San Diego, where the Pinkerton people might choose to resurrect his infamous name to make use of his reputation for their commercial purposes (and his).

Till then, he'd intended to stay dead. It had gotten old, facing down gunhands and saddle tramps who sought to steal his hard-earned, blood-soaked reputation by killing him for it. York was, after all, a dime novel hero—but he'd made not a nickel from those pen pushers' work . . . was such a thing right? Buffalo Bill had at least got a show out of it. Only a handful in the Southwest bore York's kind of gunfighter fame—Wyatt and Virgil Earp, John Wesley Hardin, Wild Bill Hickok, Bat Masterson maybe.

Circumstances had led York to an extended stay in Trinidad, with his name exposed and a badge pinned on his shirt with a couple of women who interested him encouraging an extended stay. One was Willa, a blonde Viking of a girl who could make a plaid blouse and Levis look like a wedding night.

The other was Rita Filley, and that was who burst into his office as he leaned forward in flickering lamplight, looking at dangerous ugly faces on wanted posters.

Rita's face, though tightly distraught, her usually smooth brow furrowed deep, was anything but ugly— rather, a heart-shaped home to big brown eyes, a turned-up nose, and full, red-painted lips, parted at the moment in heavy breathing. That mouth in such a condition York had witnessed before, close-up, but this was different.

The young woman, in a blue-and-gray satin gown worn in her role as hostess of the Victory Saloon, had been running, her full bosom heaving (York had witnessed that before, as well). She was otherwise slender, a striking woman whose pale complexion spoke of her Irish father but whose features recalled a Mexican mother.

She stopped in the now-open doorway, her hands propping her there, framed against the night.

"Caleb," the sultry voice panted, "you're needed at Doc Miller's!"

Rita, who had inherited the Victory from the sister whose murder York had avenged, was not to be taken lightly. Without asking of the circumstances, the sheriff rose from the hard chair, snatching the gun belt from its slumber and strapping it on as he joined the woman, who'd already stepped back outside.

Rita was on the move again. He kept up as he buckled the gun belt. Their footsteps echoed off the narrow boardwalk as they hastened.

"You remember Conchita," she huffed.

"One of your girls."

When Rita first inherited the Victory, the upstairs had been a bordello. A few months ago, at York's urging, she had converted the second floor into her own quarters and limited her girls to dance hall duties—cavorting with the cowboys and clerks, encouraging drinking, but anything beyond that was their own business . . . and not on the Victory premises.

"Working of late," he went on, "at the Red Bull. Correct?"

De Toro Rojo was a prosperous cantina in the barrio, offering spirits on the first floor and spirited *putanas* on the second. Despite a city ordinance forbidding such activity, York looked the other way. Men white and brown and black would find a place to slake their various thirsts, and not having the carnal side of things serviced at the Victory was victory enough for him.

Rita sighed and nodded, not breaking stride. "I discouraged it, but she has a child with a hungry mouth."

The night was cool, the moon full and high, Main

Street almost glowing ivory, a benign memory of a white-choked thoroughfare not so long ago. They quickly walked through this somber setting toward the three-story brick bank building.

Rita, her words rushing much as she was, said, "She was not even working tonight . . . not above. She was waiting tables, and when she refused to go upstairs with him, the bastard dragged her outside. Threw her on the ground and . . ."

Rita choked back tears.

"I get the picture," he said.

But she went on.

"He thrashed her," she said, voice trembling. "Then he . . . he ravaged her."

"You saw this?"

"No! I'd have stopped it. I'd have shot him dead. Which is what you should do, Caleb. You really should."

"Who did this?"

But Rita was already scurrying up the stairs alongside the bank building. Dr. Albert Miller's office was on the second floor. York followed Rita up to the little exterior landing and inside.

In the modest waiting room, Jonathan P. Tulley—York's deputy—was pacing like an expectant father, albeit one with a double-barreled baby in his arms already.

The bony, bandy-legged Tulley—reformed drunkard; desert rat turned deputy—was damn near resplendent in store-bought duds—flannel shirt, woolen pants, and jaunty red suspenders, the wispy head of white hair and matching beard trimmed now, with only the shapeless canvas thing that passed for a hat an echo of his prior position as town character.

"Caleb York!" the deputy blurted, coming to a sudden stop. "There be mischief afoot!"

"Mischief," a lower-pitched, calmer voice intoned from the doorway of the surgery, "is, I'm afraid, a gross understatement."

Portly little Doc Miller came in, wiping his hands with a red-splotched rag, like a bartender cleaning up after a sloppy customer. The physician was in his rolled-up shirt-sleeves, his string tie loose and limp, brown suit typically rumpled, his eyes weary behind the wire-framed glasses.

York said, his voice soft but with an edge, "What's happened to this girl?"

The sheriff stood just inside the door off the landing, with Rita at his right and Tulley having fallen in at his left, as all three faced the physician with expressions that expected the worst. They were not disappointed.

"She has been beaten to within an inch of her life," the doctor said. "Not a medical term, perhaps, but an accurate one. And that's not the worst of it."

Rita said, eyes glimmering with tears, voice filled with rage, "He attacked her! Violated her!"

Tulley was frowning. "Punishing her like that was sinful. But she lay with men for money, did she not? Ye can't say she was ruined, can ye?"

"Rape," York said, "is rape. Doc, has she said who did this?"

The physician's eyebrows rose above his glasses. "She has. The Hammond boy."

"William Hammond," York said.

It was not a question.

Hammond was the son of Victoria Hammond, widow of Andrew Hammond, a Colorado cattle baron who had died a year or so ago. His wife had, through intermediaries, been buying up the small spreads that had suffered so terribly in the Big Die-Up, and was now ensconced in the ranch house of the biggest of the smaller ranches, the Circle G.

The Hammond woman had only moved in last week and York had not yet met her. In fact, he'd had it in mind to ride out there this week, in part because of a nasty episode several nights ago involving her son, who had threatened a Bar-O cowboy with a pistol at the Victory, in an argument over one of Rita's girls.

The saloon owner had pulled in Deputy Tulley, on his night rounds, to help a bouncer of hers eject the young man—who was perhaps twenty—and give the trouble-maker a choice between a night in a cell or riding home without further incident. The boy had been arrogant and sneering (Tulley had reported to the sheriff), but accepted the latter option.

"He's a handsome boy," Rita was saying, "but a mean drunk."

Tulley said, "I was doin' my nightly rounds and Miss Rita came out of the Victory with an arm around that poor bloodied chile, walkin' her along as best she could."

Rita interjected, "She came looking for me. Needing help. Looking like stumbling death."

Tulley went on: "I helped get that poor soul to the doc's, up the stairs and within, and stood guard here while I sent Miss Rita for ye. Done the best I could, Caleb York."

"You did fine, Tulley," York said. He turned to Doc Miller. "Can I see her?"

The doc thought for a moment, then nodded. "I've given her laudanum, so she may drift off soon . . . at least I hope she will. Come with me, Caleb. . . . Rita, Tulley, stay out here, would you?"

York followed the physician through the private quarters beyond—sitting room, small kitchen, past the open doorway of the physician's bedroom and on to a spare room with a metal bed and a dresser with a basin and pitcher.

In a white hospital-style gown, Conchita was under a sheet, head sunk into a plump feather pillow. York knew her to be a pretty girl of perhaps eighteen, but that prettiness was lost under the welter of bruises and contusions, her eyes so puffy and swollen, only slits remained through which she might see. Her arms were outside the covers, exposed by short sleeves and just as heavily bruised, the impressions of strong, brutal hands left behind. Her right forearm lay at an impossible angle, as if an invisible hinge had been broken within her.

Doc nodded toward the terrible arm. "I haven't set that yet. That's next."

"Any other broken bones?"

"Some ribs. We'll bind her. She's lucky he didn't break more bones. She's lucky he didn't kill her."

"I would not call this girl lucky, Doc."

Doc's eyebrows went up. "Well . . . perhaps not. But she's lucky you're sheriff, because not all lawmen in this part of the world would take her part in this."

"But you figure I will."

"I know you will."

York approached the girl's bedside.

"Conchita," York said, leaning in, his voice a near whisper, "can you tell me the name of the one who did this?"

York already knew, of course, but he needed to hear it from her.

The girl's lips were fat with swelling, like some terrible fruit gone too ripe. "I . . . I should not have . . . said."

"No. You *should* say. You *must*."

"I was . . . crazy with pain. . . . I should . . . not have . . . said."

"Was it William Hammond, Conchita?"

"I . . . tell the doctor . . . when he ask . . . .Don't know . . . what I was saying. . . . I did not mean to say . . . The pain, it spoke for me."

"Was it the Hammond boy?"

The eye slits managed to widen. "He will . . . kill me."

"No. He won't. Conchita, do you know who I am?"

"You . . . you're the sheriff."

"I'm Caleb York. Do you know who Caleb York is?"

"He . . . you . . . famous."

"For what, Conchita?"

"For . . . killing the bad people."

"That's right. Now I want you to tell me who did this."

She did.

York took her left hand in both of his and gently squeezed. He smiled at her. She smiled back, or he thought she did. With those puffy, battered lips, who could say for sure?

Leaving the doctor to his patient and his ministrations, York joined Rita and Tulley in the waiting room. They had taken chairs but bolted to their feet upon seeing him.

"Rita, why don't you stay here for a time," York said, taking her hands in his. "Doc's got a broken wing to set and maybe he can use you at her bedside. Tulley, you and the scattergun join me. We're gonna track that boy down and talk to him some."

"I'd give 'im a good hidin', were I you, Caleb York."

"We'll try to arrest him."

Rita's eyes narrowed and she nodded to him, interpreting that in her own way.

Back out on the boardwalk, in the ivory moonlight,

the two men walked along, the tall one and the bandy-legged creature. Over to the left, the barrio mostly slept, but the glow of the Red Bull was like a fire licking at the edge of the moonlight. Outside the adobe jailhouse on this side of the street, someone was pacing, much as Tulley had been earlier, a squat figure whose footsteps made the boardwalk groan.

As the sheriff and deputy advanced, who this was became plain: Cesar, proprietor of De Toro Rojo, a hooded-eyed, bandito-mustached *hombre gordo* with wet strands of black hair plastered across his round head, whose untucked cream-color shirt and matching trousers were somehow baggy despite their wearer's size.

Cesar stopped in place, facing them as he recognized the approaching pair.

"Sheriff!" the bar owner blurted. "You are just who I wish to see!"

Rarely did the man whose business was half bar and half bordello react this favorably to Caleb York stopping in front of him.

"This *hijo de Satanás*," Cesar burst out with, "first he drag that poor *muchacha* outside *por violación*, then he come back in and he wave his gun around and bother my girls and my *cliente*."

"Did you go to that girl's aid, Cesar?"

"No. He have a gun."

York was already crossing the street, Tulley tagging along on one side, Cesar on the other.

York said to the cantina owner, "And you didn't come looking for me till he came back in and started disturbing your customers?"

"No. No."

"Did you help her in any way?"

"No. She stagger off into the night. I think to myself,

he will be satisfied now. But, no—he bother my *other* girls!"

"And your *cliente*, too, right?"

"Sí."

That was no surprise to York. He figured it would take Cesar more than one raped *prostituta* to come looking for help.

York said, "You go on ahead with Tulley and go in the back, through the kitchen. I'll take care of this, but, Tulley? You do any shooting you feel necessary."

"Happy to, Sheriff."

The deputy and the cantina owner scurried down the shabby rock-and-dirt lane separating the facing adobe hovels, raising a little dust.

By day, the humble barrio was by turns sleepy and bustling, no one in a hurry, yet somehow always in the midst of activity, chickens navigating and pecking at the space between facing adobes, mutts foraging for scraps and yapping for the hell of it. By night, no human activity at all, except trips to the privy, and the fowls penned up, the dogs curled up in doorways.

Some dogs, anyway.

At the end of this unprepossessing lane of sand-colored hovels was a two-story structure, also adobe, a shabby castle overlooking its pitiful peons. Windows blazed yellow on the first floor, and on the second windows were either dark or flickered with halfhearted candlelight. Towering faded red lettering—CANTINA DE TORO ROJO— hovered over a doorless archway.

For a moment York stopped, as gunshots from the cantina popped in the night, muffled but distinct.

York picked up his pace.

He went in, quick but studied, .44 in hand, figuring Tulley would be in position by now. The Red Bull was nothing special, as "castles" went: straw on its dirt floor, yellow walls with faded murals. Cesar's fat cigarillo-puffing wife was behind the bar, breasts bulging like cannonballs in her peasant top, a beauty mark on a plump cheek really just a mole got out of hand. Normally a confident *mujer*, she stood back away from the counter, frozen in fear. The little hombre in the big sombrero who played guitar here seemed to be trying to disappear into his corner. At the scattered mismatched tables and chairs, patrons—cowboys and town folk alike—sat motionless, not touching beers before them or the cards they'd been playing. Three señoritas in off-the-shoulder dresses were planted around the room like statues with red-rouged mouths; normally their black-and-red-and-yellow-and-green-striped skirts, petticoat plump, would be swishing around as they trolled for customers among the all-male clientele to entice upstairs.

Not tonight.

A young man who just had to be the Hammond boy sat at a table for four with a young girl on his lap, her blouse pulled down to her waist, small pert breasts exposed. Her expression was one of terror in a young life— she was perhaps fifteen—that had already taken plenty of nasty turns, and in which she had suffered more than her share of indignities. For example, right now she was having her neck nuzzled by a gun-wielding young man.

The boy was seated with his chair's back to his otherwise empty table—the other three chairs were not in use—although a bottle of tequila was within easy reach. The barrel of the Colt Single Action Army .45 in his right hand curled smoke. Across from him, on the wall, was a faded mural of a bullfighter, which now wore a number of bullet holes.

York counted them: four. So the boy had bullets left, or

at least one if the gun's owner left an empty chamber under his hammer when he carried it. But York doubted that, since this did not appear to be a cautious young man.

Rather diffidently, the boy glanced over at the newcomer. York had the .44 in hand butt at his side, meaning to display a threat only in his voice, at first.

The Hammond boy was handsome, almost too handsome. His dark hair, his dark eyes, his long, dark lashes, his pale complexion, all would have suited a woman well—a pretty boy who had probably learned to be unpretty in his ways, to make up for it. A handsome lad who'd gotten used to having women not resist his charms, although York doubted this boy had any charms that weren't physical.

And he was slender, decked out in black leather pants, a black leather vest, and a gray shirt with pearl buttons, rather like York's own.

"Put the gun down, son," York said, almost gently.

The gun, damn near too big for the boy's hand, was still pointing toward the bullfighter, though his head was turned toward York, teeth showing in a smile. White teeth.

"Don't believe I will," the boy said. "You know who I am, marshal?"

The boy had seen the badge on York's shirt.

"It's 'sheriff,' " York said. "And you've had your fun for the night."

The girl on his lap was weeping. Her hands covered her breasts.

The boy said, "Answer my question . . . Sheriff. You know who I am?"

"I know your name is Hammond. William, isn't it?"

"William, yeah. What's yours?"

"Caleb."

". . . York?"

"That's right."

The boy was still smiling but his brow had furrowed. "You're famous. A famous man. Killed people. Lot of people."

The words weren't slurred, but the speaker was drunk, all right. Capable of only a few words at a time. On the other hand, the boy had placed all four shots inside that bullfighter's torso. Assuming that's what he was aiming at.

"Son," York said, and took it up a notch, "I need you to place that gun on the table."

"Or what?"

"Suffer the consequences."

". . . Suppose I do that," the boy said. "Is that the end of it?"

"No."

"No?"

"You'll need to come with me."

"Why?"

"Because you're under arrest."

"What's the charge, Sheriff Caleb York?"

"You assaulted a young woman."

The boy's laughter was loud and harsh, and several other seated patrons responded with a jerk, as if they'd been physically slapped.

The dark, long-lashed eyes looked sleepy, but the words were wide awake: "Know where you are, Sheriff? It's a damn *cat* house! Really think you can arrest *me*? For having some cheap tart? Think I can't get away with *that*?"

York's shrug was barely perceptible. "Might be you could. For having her."

"Damn right!"

"But not for beating her senseless."

"No jury would—"

"That remains to be seen."

The smile finally disappeared.

"Now, Mr. Hammond," York said, calm but firm, "put that gun down . . . or die for it."

The boy lurched to his feet, bringing the girl along with him, making a flesh-and-blood shield out of her. He jammed the nose of the .45 in her neck, dimpling the tan flesh, and she gasped for air then held it, her eyes so wide they threatened to fall out, her mouth a terrible O too big for her face.

Tulley popped up behind the bar, in back of the boy, and yelled, "Ye best let that child go, devil spawn, or I'll splatter ye here to Sunday!"

Hammond glanced behind him, momentarily startled, then his attention returned to York. He said, "That old fool can't shoot me without taking *her* out, too! Tell him that!"

"He knows," York said quietly.

"I'm walking out of here," he said. "Right now!"

"No."

The scowl took much of his handsomeness with it. "You make way. Make way right now. I'm taking her with me. I'll let her go outside town. You come to the ranch. Tomorrow. Talk to my mother. She'll take care of things."

"No."

Now the scowl squeezed in on itself, as if tears were next. The boy, shoving the snout of the .45 deeper into the whimpering señorita's throat, yelped, "What do you mean '*no*'?"

York's .44 sent his answer, the accompanying thunder shaking the room and its inhabitants, the bullet going in clean, making a reddish black hole in William Hammond's forehead, but coming out messy, scattering brains and bone and blood like a spilled plate of Mexican food.

The girl, face spattered and speckled with red, reared away from the surprised corpse, now on its back staring at the ceiling. She flew to the arms of the nearest cowboy, who was just as surprised for a moment, then started to enjoy it, having been hugged by damn few good-looking young women, let alone one with her blouse at her waist.

Gunsmoke scorched the air as Tulley came around the bar, paused to look at the dead boy, and—shaking his head—joined York near the door.

"Hell of a shot, Sheriff," Tulley said.

York sighed and holstered his weapon. "Wish it hadn't gone that way."

"Ye don't?"

"No. For one thing, he was awful damn young to die."

"That be true, Caleb York." Tulley squinted at his boss. "But they's a *t'other* thing, is they?"

"Yes. He should have suffered more."

CHAPTER TWO

Caleb York shooed out the patrons of the cantina, not that much urging was needed. With Deputy Tulley posted outside to ward off any curious townsfolk, that left only the sheriff and Cesar, the proprietor, behind his bar helping himself to his own tequila, his plump wife having scurried out the back.

Soon the two men were joined by Trinidad's undertaker, who arrived with a callow assistant and a lidded wicker coffin. Bald, skinny C. B. Perkins managed to show up in his Abe Lincoln stovepipe and black frock coat no matter what time of day a customer turned up.

Of course, the "customer" was not really the dead young man sprawled grotesquely on the straw-strewn floor—the one who would be paying, on behalf of the county, was almost certainly the sheriff. At least that appeared to be the undertaker's assumption, based upon his first remark, the tall hat respectfully in hand.

"Would you mind, Sheriff," the undertaker's soft, midrange, uninflected voice intoned, "if I displayed this poor young wastrel's remains in my storefront window?"

York hid his irritation just barely. "I assume you intend to use the usual placard."

In fancy letters, demonstrating another of the undertaker's talents, it said, SENT TO HIS FINAL REWARD BY SHERIFF CALEB YORK. The sign had been used a number of times over these many months.

"The advertising value," Perkins said, "would help offset the modest fee the county provides."

"Your fee is unlikely to come from the county, which means you would surely be rubbing your potential client wrong."

The undertaker frowned. "Who might that client be, Sheriff?"

York nodded toward the dead young man, who was on his back, eyes wide, as if overhearing all this and keenly interested.

"This is Victoria Hammond's boy," York said. "From out at the Circle G. The widow Hammond is new to town, but I'm sure you've heard of her, and her late husband."

Eyes widened in the narrow face. "I certainly have!"

"Thought you might. She may well require one of your mahogany numbers."

Perkins, like many undertakers, was also a cabinet maker and fashioned his own caskets, as well as home furnishings. He did just as well with weddings as he did funerals. His attire was the same for either occasion.

The face stayed long and drawn, but the eyes lit up. "She might indeed. I'll call upon Mrs. Hammond tomorrow. Thank you, Sheriff, for the, uh . . ."

"Tip? Glad to help."

Perkins nodded courteously. "You're always good for business, Sheriff," he said, and then seemed to realize what he'd said, and scurried over to help his young assistant, who was also in black (apparel too large and somewhat threadbare, indicating a castoff of his employer's), in loading the corpse into the basket.

Cesar, behind the bar, darkly amused by all of this, made a gesture with his tequila bottle, in case York might like a sampling. He was considering the offer when . . .

"*Sheriff!*" a familiar voice yelped in his ear.

He managed not to jump as he turned to Tulley, suddenly at his side. "Yes, Deputy?"

Tulley's eyes were hidden behind slits in the weathered face, and he was hugging the shotgun like something dear to him, which it was. "That there scrivener's out yonder wantin' to talk to ye. Should I give him the heave-ho?"

"No, Tulley, we'll give him the respect he deserves. He's a gentleman of the press."

"Wal, he shore as hell been pressin' *me* . . . so then I take it by your words that I *am* to give him a boot in the posterior?"

"No. I mean the opposite."

Tulley blinked. "That would be right painful."

York closed his eyes briefly, opened them, and said, "I'll talk to him outside. Supervise in here."

After taking Cesar up on that shot of tequila, York went out into the cool night air, where Oscar Penniman was waiting. The editor of the weekly *Trinidad Enterprise*, a short, slight individual with wire-frame glasses on a narrow face, looked uncharacteristically rumpled in his sack coat and trousers—word of the ruckus had come to him when he was already in bed, it seemed, and he'd had to throw things on. He stood with pencil poised at notebook, his thinning hair uncombed and riding his scalp like tumbleweed.

His voice, however, was composed, a casual baritone that conveyed no judgment even if his words implied otherwise. "Another killing, Sheriff?"

"I take no pleasure in it." Perhaps, in this case, that was not entirely true, though York wasn't one to take lightly ending any man's life.

"I understand," the journalist said, "the victim is William Hammond."

"The 'victim' was resisting arrest on a serious matter."

"What matter would that be?"

York allowed himself a sigh. "There's no profit getting into that. The Hammond boy is dead and what he did to put himself at odds with the law is now between him and his maker."

Penniman cocked his head. "Word is he ravaged a girl. Thrashed her within an inch of her life."

"You have my statement. If others wish to speak to you of it, that's their lookout."

"But is it true he was holding *another* young woman hostage when you dispatched him?"

"He resisted arrest, wielding a weapon. That's enough for your purposes, Penniman."

"Do you fear retribution from the Hammonds?"

He narrowed his eyes at the man. "That's all I have to say on the matter. Be on your way."

Penniman smiled and shrugged. "They're a powerful family, Sheriff. The late Andrew was a terror, they say. Ruthless. And rumor is his widow is cut from the same cloth. How do you imagine she will take to you sending her youngest son to Kingdom Come?"

"My deputy wants to send *you* on your way with a kick in the backside. Should I summon him?"

Penniman raised a single hand of surrender and he and his notebook headed back into the night. As he did, he passed by another figure, headed York's way, another small if stouter individual wearing a derby and cutaway jacket;

about fifty, the man sported a graying handlebar mustache. He was no one York recognized.

"You're Caleb York, I believe," he said, approaching, doffing his hat.

"I can confirm that belief," York said.

"I understand there's been a shooting."

"If that were the case, how would that be your concern?"

He half bowed. "Alfred Byers. I'm bookkeeper and general factotum out at the Circle G. I was bucking the tiger over at the Victory this evening."

Poker was the preferred game at the Victory Saloon, but there was often a faro table going as well. Not York's preference, which might be why he hadn't encountered Byers yet, as "bucking the tiger" referred to faro, not poker.

The stout little bookkeeper was saying, "I hear there's been a tragedy involving young Hammond. Is that truly the case?"

As if in answer to that question, the undertaker and his associate came out of the De Toro Rojo lugging the wicker coffin, excusing themselves, and York and Byers stepped aside.

"Hold up," York said.

Perkins and his helper paused.

"Set it down," York added.

They did.

Then to Byers, York said, "Would you mind formally identifying the deceased?"

Holding the derby to his belly, Byers nodded and the undertaker lifted the lid.

"That's William Hammond," the bookkeeper said. His voice betrayed nothing. Then to undertaker Perkins, he said, "Sir, I represent the Hammond interests. We will be in touch. Are you a purveyor of the embalming arts?"

Post-Civil War, many morticians were.

But Perkins said, "I am not, sir."

Byers thought for a moment. "Do you have ice the young man can rest upon for the time being? We will want to arrange a service and the boy's brothers will likely be coming from out of town."

"Certainly. Perhaps you would like to have someone come around to select a casket?"

"Not necessary. Just make it the best you have."

Perkins tipped his stovepipe and said, "The very best indeed, sir," and then he and the boy in the undertaker's cast-off clothes lugged the grisly remains in the picnic basket of a coffin down the street. Perkins was having difficulty curtailing a smile. William Hammond's bad night had been a very good one for C. B. Perkins.

Soon William Hammond would have mahogany and brass fittings, York knew, not that it would matter to the boy.

Byers put his derby back on and, polite, even cordial, asked, "Might I know the circumstances of young Hammond's passing?"

"He ravaged and beat a young woman senseless. When I requested he give himself up, he made a hostage of another girl and I shot him dead."

The bookkeeper nodded, as if that were just so many more figures to record in his mental ledger. "The young man had his problems. No doubt he'd been imbibing."

"No doubt. But I'd imagine you had a few tonight, playing faro, and managed not to ravage and batter any young women—at least none that have come to my attention."

"True. True."

York met the man's eyes earnestly. "Is it too late for me to ride out to the Circle G to speak to the boy's mother? It's my responsibility to deliver the sad tidings."

"I'm sure Mrs. Hammond will wish to speak to you about the matter."

York thought, *I bet she will.*

Byers continued: "But the news will be better coming from me. I'll convey the gist of tonight's tragedy, and report the arrangements I've made with . . . what is the mortician's name?"

"Perkins. The only one in town."

"Not surprising. It's a small town."

"But lively," York commented. "I'll be out to the G midmorning, if that seems suitable."

"That will be fine."

"Do tell Mrs. Hammond that I regret this affair worked out in such a fashion. Assure her I did my best to bring her boy in alive."

He sighed, nodded. "It's not the first incident involving young William, I'm afraid," the bookkeeper said.

And he tipped the derby and went off into the night.

But it will be the last, York thought. *For William Hammond, anyway.*

What steps his mother and brothers might take remained to be seen.

Under a sun still making its climb, Caleb York rode his black-maned, dappled gray gelding up the narrow rutted road that cut through the flat expanse beyond Trinidad. Here and there on either side shimmered occasional pools of fetid water, and even on the somewhat soft roadway itself a few puddles remained.

The aftermath of the brutally hard blizzards that had shown up like one unwanted guest after another further displayed itself in the leaning telegraph poles and battered-looking cacti, as well as squashed yucca and stripped pinyon pines. The occasional juniper tree, bereft of green, was left with its thick, gnarled branches reaching for the sky like the limbs of dying animals. On the nearby range, still-rotting corpses of cattle would have a similar look of terror and tragedy.

Five minutes or so from town, off to the right, came the inaccurately named Boot Hill—it was just as flat as any of the surrounding landscape—where wooden crosses and tombstones struck odd angles or had even fallen over, the mesquites that normally shaded the cemetery wearing many a partial, snapped-off branch. About the only unaffected aspect of the view was the shelf of distant burnt-red buttes with their weather-scarred cliff sides.

York faced a first-time duty this morning in this lawman's job he'd held for going on a year. Oh, he had informed a parent here and a spouse there of the accidental death of a loved one—this one thrown from a horse, that one bit by a rattler. In the Southwest, the only thing cheaper than life was death. But never before had he had to face the mother of a man—a boy, in this case—whom he had killed.

He had killed too many men, and too many had been boys or nearly so, wanting to shoot him and stake a claim on his reputation. But this was a region and a time when men (and women, too) disappeared into the geography, changing names, inventing new personas, abandoning lives lived elsewhere, including crimes committed in those jettisoned years, even inventing lives never lived at all. The clerk in New Mexico might have been a murderer in New York. The housewife in Texas might have been a prostitute in Kansas. The deputy in Arizona may have robbed a stage in California.

Who was Billy the Kid, really? William Bonney? Or Henry McCarty? Maybe Kid Antrim? And that was just a single twenty-one-year life. Yet even with an infamous character like the Kid, no one really cared who he'd really once been.

The dead were as anonymous as the living.

That Byers character had done the sheriff a favor by taking the news to the Hammond woman. Breaking it to her himself was not something he'd have relished. Few things in life did Caleb York shy away from—no challenge, no responsibility, no danger . . . he could face just about anything. He took pride in that.

But the mother of a boy he'd killed, however much that terrible child deserved it? York shivered, even as he tried to write it off to a chill morning. But it wasn't *that* chill today, as he damn well knew.

For that reason—and this was another first—York was going out on official business unheeled, his Colt Single Action .44 and gun belt left behind at his jailhouse office. He could not bring himself to wear the weapon he'd used to kill the boy to a meeting with the mother. Not that he was unarmed—his double-barreled twelve-gauge shotgun was in its saddle scabbard.

But it would stay outside and York would go in.

He wore black, though not in mourning—the cavalry pinch hat, coat, pants, boots, string tie, all black, his gray shirt an exception only by a shade. He was a professional man, in his view, as much so as a doctor or lawyer.

Beyond the boneyard, and before the Bar-O's log arch announced the lane to the Cullen ranch, a trail veered off to the right, leading to the Circle G. Even before the hard winter, the going had been rough on this narrow lane, and anything but scenic—the bunch grass and spiny shrubs had a stomped-on, defeated look. Afterwhile, though, some green came in and soon ahead loomed the squared-off, fence-post archway with its circled G burned into a wooden overhang.

The array of frame buildings—water tower, barn, cookhouse, bunkhouse—was set in and around a backdrop of tall firs that had withstood the wintery onslaught. They were the towering beneficiaries of Sugar Creek, a nearby offshoot of the Purgatory River.

A single corral, absent of men and horses, indicated the Circle G was—although second only to the Bar-O of the ranches surrounding Trinidad—a modest affair. Yet the ranch house itself belied that, a sprawling one-story adobe structure with a half-story, sloping faded-green roof that gave it stature, with matching shutters and, beneath the overhang, a colonnade. York had been inside when others lived here, and knew a courtyard lent the place a real hacienda feel. He'd been told Casa Guerrero dated to the 1830s when a Mexican cattle rancher had built it before the latest corrupt government sold the place out from under him to Americanos.

As York rode in past a cottonwood that shaded the house and seemed none the worse for wear from the rough winter, Byers—who had obviously been keeping watch for him—emerged from the house, the bookkeeper's expression pleasant, almost friendly. As York tied the gelding up at the hitching post, Byers approached, coming down the two steps from the low-slung porch.

"You're a man of your word," Byers said, extending his hand. "Not that I'm surprised."

They shook.

York asked, "How did your mistress take it?"

"She doesn't show much in any situation. Any crying was behind closed doors. If she has anger toward you, she hasn't shown it. . . . Step inside, won't you, Sheriff? Mrs. Hammond is waiting in the library."

York followed the bookkeeper into a world of low open-beamed ceilings, white walls, archways, dark finely crafted furnishings, and colorful Mexican throw carpets on polished wood floors, all much as York remembered from previous visits, with the only change the removal of paintings and statues of the Catholic faith in favor of landscapes of the American West.

As they moved through a living room, with a fireplace and overstuffed seating, York said, "I understand you've acted as a sort of advance man for Mrs. Hammond."

"Yes, I've been here for a month or so. Putting things in order. And in motion."

"Buying up some of the smaller spreads, I understand."

Byers paused at a closed windowless door, vertically paneled oak and heavy looking. "In the aftermath of any tragedy, there are . . . opportunities. People need to sell out and move on. Other more . . . hearty, resilient souls are left to . . ." Byers searched for the word.

York grinned and said, "Take advantage?"

Byers's smile was honest, anyway. "It's the way of the world, Sheriff. I would imagine a man who has lived your rather storied life has no illusions otherwise. . . . Excuse me."

Byers opened the door just enough to squeeze through, leaving it ajar as he said, "Mrs. Hammond, the sheriff is here."

The response came immediately, and the voice was a throaty purr. "Send him in please, Alfred."

Byers emerged with a mild smile, gestured with an open hand, and opened the door. Hat in hand, York stepped in and Byers closed the door behind the caller.

York found himself in what had been described as a library but was more a den. Two facing bookcases each hugged a side wall, not the built-in expectation, with eight shelves between them. The volumes, at a glance, seemed largely business oriented, although York did catch the spines of two novels—*Ben-Hur* by the territory's former governor, and *The Adventures of Huckleberry Finn*—both of which the sheriff (though not an avid reader) had made it through.

At the far end of the room hung a huge oil painting, a standing portrait that York recognized as the late Andrew Hammond, a tall, burly figure in muttonchops with a severe look and a firm jaw. He was dressed in a fine cutaway suit with cravat, but had been known to dress like a cowhand when among his men or out carousing.

York knew him only by reputation, though the stories and illustrations of him in the press were familiar to most in the West—certainly to every lawman, since Hammond's sizable spread in Colorado was rumored—hell, was *known*—to have been built on stock rustled below the border by the Cowboys, the now-defunct criminal gang that the Earp brothers took on in Tombstone a few years before.

The white walls were otherwise taken up by even more Western landscapes, a few of which included Indian subjects; all had fancy gilded frames. An Oriental rug was flung on the polished wood floor at an odd angle, like a discarded flying carpet, but it managed to serve as a home for two comfortable black leather button-tufted chairs that faced a massive walnut desk with brass fittings, beautifully carved in the Spanish fashion.

The woman seated at the desk had features every bit as beautifully carved, her cheekbones high, her eyes large

and so dark brown as to be almost black, her nose aqui-
line, her lips rather thin but with a lovely symmetry, the
cleft between nose and upper lip well defined. The effect
was that God had really taken His time designing this
particular Eve.

Her native beauty was enhanced by a black lace dress
with mantilla, under which her black hair was up; her
black-gloved hands were folded before her, both business-
like and prayerful. She was in mourning, all right, but
only some red filigree in the whites of her eyes suggested
the sorrow she must have experienced through a long
night.

"Mrs. Hammond, you have my sympathy for your
loss, and my apologies for not coming personally last
night. I am usually not prone to cowardice."

She unfolded her hands just long enough to gesture to
one of the chairs opposite. He settled into it, placing his
hat on the desktop, which was otherwise bare.

"You were right not to come," the low, throaty voice
intoned. "Mr. Byers requested that you allow *him* to
bring word, and that was proper. You are, after all, the
person who . . . dealt with William last night."

"I am."

"For both of us to have to share the delivery of that
news would have added mutual discomfort . . . don't you
think?"

"Yes. But it's kind of you to have *any* thought for my
feelings."

A tiny, fleeting smile. "I admit to thinking more of myself in that regard."

York shifted in the chair. He could smell her—or her
perfume or maybe the aftermath of her bath . . . lilacs.
She was lovely, this mother of the boy he killed last night.

He said, "If you wish the details, I will share them. I warn you they are unpleasant, but you have a right to hear of it from—"

She raised a silencing hand, a gentle gesture, yet firm. "That is not necessary. Mr. Byers has taken care of that."

"Mr. Byers was not there."

"No. But I feel he conveyed the facts adequately." She leaned forward; the dark eyes behind the lace curtain of the mantilla were strangely warm. "You must understand, Caleb . . . may I call you 'Caleb'? I have heard and read enough about you that I feel I almost know you."

"If you wish. Certainly."

Perhaps tellingly, she did not ask him to call her Victoria.

"Caleb, I have three sons, or I should say, I had three, and now two remain—a pair of fine young men, each of whom runs a family business. My eldest son, Hugh, is the president of our bank in your sister city, in Colorado . . ."

Colorado had a Trinidad, too.

". . . and my middle boy, Pierce, looks after our ranching interests in those same parts. I had hoped, one day, that William might gain the maturity to take over the management of this ranch. It was not to be."

"I *am* sorry." Not for what he'd done, but for having to do it.

Her head tilted to one side. "I fear William's fate was inevitable. If not you, it would have been someone else. If I might be frank?"

"If you like."

"There had been many difficulties with my youngest son. He was a smart, sweet boy, which you may find difficult to believe. But he bore the curse of drink, something his late father shared with the youth, although

Andrew had tamed that beast. After many wild years that, frankly, took considerable forbearance from me, my late husband gave up drink. He had achieved a certain respectability that went with the wealth he accumulated and he wanted to maintain both."

"I see."

Her husband's reputation had been for building and maintaining his cattle ranch with beef rustled from Mexico. But under the circumstances, York let that pass.

"Make no mistake," she said, chin high, "I will mourn my son. I will cherish his memory and, as mothers do, sweep aside his failings into some untended, rarely visited corner of my memory. But I hold you in no way responsible."

"Very gracious of you, ma'am."

Her smile was sad but it was indeed a smile. "Am I so much older than you? Must it be 'ma'am'? You haven't seen forty yet, and if I *have*, it's not yet retreated into the distance."

"If I am not out of line saying so," York said carefully, "in this hacienda you are the image of the graceful señoritas who must once have dwelled here."

"You have a poetic way," she said, "for a gunfighter."

That word—"gunfighter"—had just the slightest edge.

"But," she said, "I am no señorita. That's a happenstance of this dwelling I purchased. My mother came from Belfast and she and my father met in San Francisco, where they were both doing business. You may interpret that as you will."

That didn't seem to York to need much interpretation, although he couldn't imagine why she'd be so frank with him, the small-town sheriff who killed her son.

She answered the question in his eyes. "Sheriff, my

son's tragic passing has brought us together, but we do not have to be adversaries. You're aware that Mr. Byers, as my agent, has been purchasing the smaller spreads in the vicinity."

"I am."

"Do you have any idea why?"

He shrugged. "I would assume that farther north, in our sister city and thereabouts up in Colorado, you got hit even harder by the blizzards."

Her nod was slow. "We did. That is a fact. What little stock survived we sold, and we divested ourselves of several other Colorado properties, and purchased this spread from the Gauge family, who had no interest in pursuing this difficult means of livelihood, and were only too happy to sell out reasonably."

"The pickings here were favorable, I'm sure."

"We mean to brazen it out, Caleb. To rebuild the cattle industry into something like what it was, before Mother Nature took her stern hand. It's not a game for cowards or the weak."

He gestured with an open hand. "Others are going a different way. Merging cattle ranching and farming on much smaller spreads. You aim to put together something grander, I take it?"

The big dark eyes got bigger. "I do. My youngest son is a casualty of his own weaknesses and of a part of the country where men carry guns to the grocer's and church. My other sons will live to see this place become civilized, and, God willing, so will I."

"In my official capacity," York said, with a shrug, "I will do what I can to help."

"That I am glad to hear. But you may be wondering why, under these grave circumstances, I might subject you to a lecture on the subject of the future of the Hammond family cattle business."

"Meaning no disrespect," York said, "I think you might feel you have me at a disadvantage. If there would ever be a time I'd be beholden to you, this would be it."

She smiled again. She made a sound that was almost a laugh and not quite a grunt. "You are not wrong. But what I mostly want to do is make sure—despite the tragic circumstance—that we do not . . . get off on the wrong foot."

York wondered how much farther on the wrong foot one might get than to shoot and kill someone's son.

"I had already," she said, head back, "made something of a study of you, from a distance. Mr. Byers made some inquiries—discreetly."

That straightened him. "In what regard?"

"You were a close confidant of the late George Cullen. And you are friendly with his daughter."

"Yes." He chose not to explore the precise meaning of "friendly" in this context.

"Willa Cullen is young, I understand. Twenty-three, twenty-four?"

"Twenty-three."

"Very young to be running a cattle ranch, and right now she—like so many others, after the blizzard—is in a most precarious position."

"She's a strong young woman."

The Hammond woman leaned on her elbows. "So I understand. But I hope to buy her out. With the Bar-O merging with the Circle G, and all of the smaller ranches I've acquired, mine will be the biggest operation in the Territory."

Not *would* be—*will* be.

"Miss Cullen," York said, "grew up on that ranch. She was George Cullen's only child. She views herself as the equivalent of her father's son. I *do* know her well, and I doubt you could tempt her."

She seemed to take no offense. "As I say, I had some discreet inquiries around Trinidad made about you, Caleb. If anyone could . . . *tempt* her . . . it might well be you."

That didn't sit well with him. He rose. "Again, Mrs. Hammond, you have my sympathies."

The throaty voice grew just a little louder. "She grew up in that house, you say—well, she could have it. She could stay there. Perhaps we might set aside some farmland. My sole interest is in cattle."

More so than her dead son, it would seem.

"If you feel I'm owed any debt," she said coolly, "in the tragedy that brought you here, perhaps you would consider speaking to Miss Cullen on my behalf. Who knows? Perhaps Caleb York could persuade her to sell— that doing so would be in her best interests."

Was he reading a threat in that?

His hostess rose, came around the desk, and took him by the arm—this seemed her way of dismissing him, benignly. She was taller than he'd figured, and as graceful as he'd imagined, and the black dress hugged her rather curvaceous figure like an overeager suitor. This woman of perhaps forty could have made a much younger man drunk with her beauty.

"We won't be adversaries, Sheriff York," she said. "You're the most famous man in the New Mexico Territory, after all."

And would she soon be the most famous woman? York wondered. *Was that her implication?*

She deposited him in the hall, sealed herself back in her chamber, and Byers materialized to show him out.

"Remarkable woman, don't you think?" the bookkeeper asked.

"Well, I'll say one thing."

"Yes?"

"She's holding up."

CHAPTER THREE

Willa Cullen guided the buckboard drawn by two quarter horses under the log arch with the chain-hung plaque boldly bearing a big burnt O—echoing the Bar-O brand.

The lovely young woman looked tomboyish in her red-and-black plaid shirt and denims and boots, but no less feminine for it. The tall, shapely girl wore her straw-yellow hair up and braided in back, which went well with her long-lashed, cornflower-blue eyes.

This late morning she was accompanied by lanky, weathered stockman Lou Morgan, who had helped her on the supply run into Trinidad for flour, sugar, beans, lard, molasses, coffee, and rice, plus bacon packed in bran and eggs in cornmeal. Even with a reduced number of cowhands, it took a lot to keep a ranch going like the one she'd inherited not so long ago.

The largest spread around, the Bar-O boasted a corral, two barns, rat-proof grain crib, log bunkhouse, and cookhouse with hand pump, wooden bench, and row of tin wash basins along an awning-shaded porch. The ranch house was a rambling log-and-stone affair that had been added onto several times, the central wooden structure with its plank-wood front porch erected by her late father in pioneering days.

But for a swirl of smoke from the cookhouse, things looked deserted, with the herders out on their grim duties—for weeks now, about half of Willa's buckaroos were keeping watch on the skinny few thousand surviving beeves, the other hands still gathering bloated carcasses to pile up in ghastly barbecues, fighting off buzzards and wolves to do so.

About half of her hands had moved on—some had up and quit; a few had died in the last brutal blizzard. She had been impressed by how many of the colored cowboys and Mexican vaqueros had stuck despite hard going. Her current foreman, Bill Jackson, was an ex-slave from Mississippi, and didn't seem easily thrown by anything life threw at him. Help like that in times like these was priceless.

Willa's visitor might have been lost in the rustic landscape, but she picked him out at once—Caleb York, sitting on the front steps, hat in his hand, looking in his usual black like a handsome, rawboned preacher come calling. His dappled gray gelding, with its distinctive black mane, was hitched nearby, black tail twitching.

As she approached, guiding the buckboard toward the house, Caleb rose and smiled shyly and waved. Seeing him sent something leaping in her—that often happened, but because she'd earlier been disappointed at his absence in town, the sensation felt keener.

Back in Trinidad, while Morgan and the proprietor's slow-witted son Lem piled the sacks in back of the buckboard outside Harris Mercantile, Willa had headed up the boardwalk to the sheriff's office, hoping to find Caleb at his desk.

Instead she'd found Deputy Jonathan P. Tulley sitting at *his* "desk"—a rough-hewn table overseen by wanted posters and a rifle rack near the wood-burning stove, which was going just enough to keep a pot of coffee warm. She helped herself to the chair behind the absent Caleb's desk—the familiarity had been earned.

"Sleeping in, is he?" she said.

"Not hardly. Coffee, miss?"

"No thanks." She'd experienced Tulley's coffee before. The deputy was saying, "He's out to the Circle G."

She sat up. "What business has he there?"

"Callin' on the Hammond woman. Kilt her boy last night."

Now she really sat up. "*What?*"

Tulley told the tale, in a colorful way almost worth sharing.

When he wrapped up his account, Tulley asked, "Have ye met the widow Hammond yet?"

"No."

Tulley clicked in his cheek. "I hear she's a fine figger of a female. Word is she's buyin' up all them small spreads in your neck of the woods."

"So I hear. But I also hear she's taken on some rough cowboys."

". . . Cowboys like them that rode with the Clantons and McLauries?"

"That's right." She sighed. "I hope Caleb knows what he's doing."

"Generally does. He only kilt that boy 'cause that's what you do with mad dogs. How is things out to the Bar-O, since the Die-Up?"

"Taxing. Ugly."

"Sheriff's gettin' a house, I hear." He looked at her with a twinkle. "Mayhap ye should move to town. Cattle ranchin' is no fit trade for the gentler sex."

She got up and went over and grabbed him by his suspenders and yanked him bug-eyed to his feet. " 'Mayhap' you should mind your own business, Deputy Tulley."

She let go of him and the sounds of his suspenders snapping and him sitting hard in his wooden chair foreshadowed her slamming of the jailhouse door.

Looking back on that, in the buckboard, she felt foolish. Tulley hadn't meant any harm—he seldom did, unless wielding a shotgun at the sheriff's behest.

And now here Caleb was, on her literal doorstep! Tulley had been wrong—the sheriff had ridden out to see *her*, not the high-and-mighty Victoria Hammond.

Caleb came over and helped her down from the buckboard—she didn't need the help, of course, but it was gentlemanly of him. The jangle of harness announced Lou was heading over to the cookhouse to start unloading the cookie's share of supplies.

"Willa," he said, smiling.

"Caleb," she said, smiling back. "Why am I honored with this visit? Your deputy said you were going out to see the Hammond woman."

His gaze lowered. "I was. I needed to convey my sympathies."

"For killing her son?"

"Yes. For killing her son."

The buckboard was whining under the unloading down at the cookhouse, Harmon, the plump whitebearded cook, lending a hand.

"From what Tulley told me," she said, "the boy had it coming. . . . Care to sit for a while? I made lemonade this morning."

"Best offer I've had today."

She was glad to hear that.

When they were inside, with the door shut, Caleb put his hat and coat on the wall pegs, then took her in his arms and kissed her. The kiss, and the embrace that went with it, lasted a while. They were alone in the house—she had no servant, unless you counted Caleb York. Then she took him by the hand and walked him into and across the living room.

The narrowness of the room made it seem longer and larger than it was, the fittings a mix of her late parents— her mother's finely carved Spanish-style furnishings and her father's hand-hewn, bark-and-all carpentry that went well with the hides on the floor and mounted antler heads. An imposing stone fireplace seemed protected by a pair of Winchesters—a Model 1866 and a Model 1855— working relics from her papa's pioneer past, each supported by mounted upturned deer hoofs.

In front of the unlit fireplace were positioned twin homemade chairs, good size, with folded-over Indian blankets serving as cushions; Caleb sat. She fetched him a mason jar of lemonade, and one for herself as well, and settled into the other chair. A rough-hewn table fashioned by George Cullen separated them.

"How did she take it?" Willa asked him.

"I don't really know."

"You . . . ?"

He shrugged, sipped lemonade. "She has a bookkeeper and . . . 'factotum' he calls himself, name of Byers, who came by last night and got the particulars. Took the word out to her."

"I've met Byers. He seems too nice to trust."

Caleb twitched a smile. "I sensed that myself. The clean man who does the dirty work."

"Then you went there, strictly to . . ."

"Pay my respects." He sipped more lemonade. "You make a mean glass of this stuff. Very nice. Tart."

"She's a very nice tart, you say? Victoria Hammond?"

That made him outright smile, but he said, "Don't be unkind. She lost her son."

"Word is he was a drunken lout and, after all, he ravaged and thrashed that poor girl, if Tulley's to be believed."

"He's generally reliable. The whelp forced me into killing him, so I won't lose sleep. Still. Sitting across from the deceased's mother was unsettling."

"She gave you what for?"

"Not at all." He told her how the mother had spoken openly of her son's failings and even those of her late husband. "She was very frank."

"It may have been a device."

"How so?"

Willa sipped her lemonade; she felt she hadn't made it sweet enough, but it would have to do. "My understanding is the woman has taken on some of the lowest-down cowhands in the Southwest. Brigands and gunfighters, rabble left over from Tombstone days."

"I've heard that too," he admitted.

"And the way her husband made himself a cattle baron was by buying beef rustled from Mexico." She rolled her eyes. "Situated here, all the closer to the border, I can well imagine we'll have a cattle *baroness* soon, doing much the same."

His eyebrows flicked up and down. "If so, and if the Mexican authorities want my help, I will pitch in. But it's not my place to do anything in San Miguel County, unless they rustle from you or the other ranchers around. Is that your concern?"

She laughed and it was bitter enough to make the lemonade seem sweet. "What cattle is there to rustle? My poor scrawny things? There'll be no roundup this year, and I'll have to find a way to fatten them up to make it next season. No, Victoria Hammond will be following her late husband's lead by taking on beef below the border, where they didn't get hit by the blizzards."

This time his eyebrows stayed up a while. "Maybe you should consider selling out to her. She's buying. She said so."

Willa frowned. "I *know* she's buying. She's grabbed half a dozen of the small spreads, at bargain rates." She looked at him, hard. "Did she ask you to . . . Caleb, are you her damn *messenger*?"

He winced at that. "She did ask me to approach you, yes . . . but that's not what I'm doing."

"Isn't it?"

"No. I'm just telling what she told me. What her intentions are. I didn't get the sense she wanted to take advantage of you, even if she has done, where some of the smaller ranchers are concerned."

She stood.

Came over and planted herself in front of him and put her hands on her hips, her legs apart, a female Colossus of Rhodes.

"You really don't *know*, do you, Caleb York?"

"What don't I know?"

"She's liable to make me an offer so paltry the other deals her man Byers wangled will make her look the soul of generosity. She thinks she has me at a disadvantage, and . . . and maybe she does."

She sighed and joined him in the big rugged chair. He slipped an arm around her shoulders and she sat in his lap with her head on his chest like he was Daddy.

Her laugh was almost a moan. "You really don't know anything about cattle, do you, Caleb?"

"No."

"Aren't interested in the least."

"No. Well. I'm interested in a certain cattle rancher, but . . . no. My interest in beef stops when I cut into a thick steak and hope to find it nice and bloody. Tender, too, preferably."

"Oh, you like them tender, do you?"

"I do."

She kissed him. He kissed her.

"What this is about," she told him, and she may have been in Daddy's lap but he was the child being lectured, "is Sugar Creek."

"It is? The stream with all the white sand, you mean."

She looked up at him and nodded. "Which is why it's called Sugar Creek, most likely, yes. It's on Victoria Hammond's property. It's practically in her backyard."

"What's important about some little crick? You have a *river* running through your land."

"The Purgatory River, yes. And what's the Purgatory River like right now?"

He thought about it. "Fouled by rotting cattle carcasses . . . clogged with death and decay. We're lucky we have wells in town, because that polluted stuff's not fit to drink."

"For man . . . nor beast."

His head went back. "Oh. You're saying, right now she has the only source in these parts for clean water . . . for *anybody's* herd."

"Yes. We never put anything in writing, any of us cattle ranchers. But Papa never asked anything for sharing the Purgatory's clean water with his neighbors. Likewise any cattlemen who wanted their beef to partake of Sugar Creek were free to do so, with their neighbor's blessing. Byers brought word to me that the Hammonds did not feel obliged to honor that understanding. Sugar Creek was theirs."

Caleb's features had turned stony. "That woman thought I'd do her bidding for her . . . with you. She thought she could hold that boy's killing over my head and make me come to you and. . . . What the hell kind of woman uses her son's death to gain a business advantage?"

Neither of them said anything for a while.

She curled up in his arms and managed not to cry. She would have hated herself for that. Caleb would not have held it against her, would not have seen anything female or weak about it—he was not that kind of man.

But she knew she had to be strong in the fight with Victoria Hammond that lay ahead.

They sat nestled before the stone fireplace as if it were warm and not just a cold well-arranged pile of stones, and finally she rose and held out her hand and led him to her bedroom.

They had become very intimate during the blizzard,

and what followed had become an event if not regular, not infrequent, either.

Perhaps half an hour later, in her metal-post double bedstead, they lay under a cool sheet together with a light blanket at their middle, and he said, "Even with all the land that woman has grabbed up, her property pales next to yours. She covets the Bar-O—she wants it for herself, to make the Circle G the biggest cattle outfit in the Territory. She said so."

"She can go jump."

"You can make her jump, Willa. She has Sugar Creek, but you have all this range. Squeeze her dry."

"She can make me the dry one."

"I say you still have the advantage. You want some water rights—temporary at that, because the Purgatory won't always be fouled. She wants . . . everything."

The mistress of the Bar-O leaned on an elbow. The sheet fell to her waist and her pert breasts were exposed and she didn't care a whit. She was comfortable with this man, and she wasn't some fool female who had to undress in the dark with her mate.

And that's what he was. It wasn't official yet, but that's what he was. Her mate.

He was propped on an elbow, too. He grinned at her. "Listen, darling child. You'll have money coming in from the railroad, for the right-of-way you're granting—now that spring's here, they'll be putting track down soon."

"They will," she said, nodding. "That at least is a blessing."

"And I'm gonna be well fixed, you know I am. I'll co-own the train station with Raymond Parker, thanks to the land your papa left me. Trinidad will boom before long, and I'm the county sheriff *and* the acting marshal now. How about that?"

She curled her fingers in the hair on his chest. "I guess I can put up with having a rich husband."

"Good. Because as tax collector, I get a nice cut, plus my share of rewards for outlaws too dumb to know what it means to face Caleb York down. They're providing use of a house, you know."

She smiled a little, amused by how talkative the normally taciturn Caleb York could be in her bedroom. "You don't need a house," she told him. "I have a house."

"Well, we can have two houses, or maybe we'll sell yours and—"

The smile went away. "If I sell out to that witch, why would I have my house?"

He shrugged. "She said you could keep it. Could keep enough land to farm a little, as well. She just wants the range, and what's left of your cattle."

"Oh, is that all she wants?"

"I can only tell you what she told me. But if you have this place, it's not so far out of town that I couldn't put down stakes here. Ride back and forth."

Her brow furrowed. "Caleb . . . if . . . when . . . we marry . . . you intend to stay a lawman?"

"I do. Money will roll in from the train station and I'll invest in businesses in town. A man can't be a gunfighter forever."

"But as long as you wear a badge . . . two badges . . . young fools like William Hammond will face you down. And some day one will be quicker than you or a better shot or just . . . luckier than you."

His smile said he didn't take the threat of that seriously. "Sweetheart, the West is changing. Blink and a new century will be at our feet."

She was shaking her head. "Don't you see, Caleb? You can live here with me. Into the next century. We can run this *ranch* as a business. A smaller herd, with fenced-in grazing . . . some farming. No cowboying for you. No fixing fences or riding herd or roping runaways."

"That's not the future your father imagined for the Bar-O."

"No, but he never suffered a winter the likes of what we did. And what I'm talking about is real. It's practical. And it's not dangerous. No drunken boys with six-shooters to deal with, or brothers of men who you justly sent to hell. Just me and you and . . . a family."

He didn't respond at once. He was digesting it.

"I do want a family with you," he said finally. "But I'm not a rancher. I'm not a farmer." His gaze intensified. "Do you know where I grew up?"

He had never told her.

"No," she said.

"Ohio. My father was a farmer. He struggled, he near broke his back toiling, and he never got anywhere. I worked in his fields and I hated it. I hated it. Long, hard, punishing days for nothing. When I had the chance to en-list, just a boy really, I joined the Union Army and I killed Confederates. Then they sent me west and I killed the Red Indian in my blue uniform. I'm not sure anybody I killed deserved it, grayback or redskin, but I learned how, all right. To kill. To use guns."

"Caleb . . ."

He was out of the bed and getting into his clothes, now.

"I got a job with Wells Fargo and I fell into man hunt-ing. I was still a killer, but I became a detective, too, which is a better trade than soldier. I didn't mind tracking down Southern boys when they'd robbed or killed, or In-dians when they'd done bad things also. Didn't mind tak-ing their lives if they tried to take mine. It made what I did not so . . . horrible."

He was pulling on his boots. She had never heard him say so much all at once.

"So that's who I am, darling girl. I am a man who would rather kill than farm. Who would much rather eat beef than raise it."

She was still naked and he was fully dressed when he leaned in and said, not without humor, "This is what we call in my trade a Mexican standoff."

Then he was gone.

CHAPTER FOUR

Shortly after Caleb York left the library at the Circle G, Victoria Hammond—her features set in a scowl that challenged their loveliness—called for Byers.

"Yes, ma'am?" he said from the doorway. The stout little bookkeeper was trained to know that half of the time his mistress wanted an errand and the other half desired his presence at her desk for business. Only in the latter case would he enter the chamber.

This was an errand.

She asked, "Is Mr. Colman with the contingent at the creek?"

"Yes, Mrs. Hammond. He and half a dozen armed men are positioned there. They've set up camp."

That was less than a mile away.

"Send for him," she said.

"Yes, ma'am."

Her black lace–gloved hands were spread apart, clenched very tight, as if she were a child about to beat her fists on the desktop in a tantrum. But tantrums were not something Victoria Hammond allowed herself. Still, it had taken all of her self-control to withhold the depth of her feelings, to quell the extent of her hatred, while the Trinidad sheriff who had slaughtered her boy was in her presence.

William had been flawed, as were all human beings. But he was her son. The sheriff should have known that the progeny of Victoria Hammond, who was already an important landowner in his county, should have been handled with care. With courtesy. With forbearance. For William to lose his life over some slatternly Mexican wench was a travesty of justice.

Victoria Hammond's definition of justice, as with so many in the Southwest after the war between North and South, was part of a personal code derived from family and business concerns, and had little to do with anything to be found in law books.

She had grown up in a bordello—her mother, Irene McCalley, was among the first madams in San Francisco—with dozens of soiled doves as her surrogate sisters. Her father was Jack Daley, her mother's common-law husband, who ran a Barbary Coast gambling hall. Her mother's place had been a plush parlor house, her father's a wide-open saloon, and both catered to clientele that included judges, senators, and a governor or two. By the time she was eight, her parents had moved to Nob Hill and she was enrolled in various all-girl schools locally, all Catholic of course, instilling in her a disdain for religion that had only grown in time.

Not yet twenty, she was courted by Andrew Hammond, a Wyoming cattleman who had started out her father's valued customer, then became his best friend, and finally business partner. But after the Frisco vigilantes strung up her father and drove her mother to suicide, with the collective fortune of her parents swallowed up by a corrupt local government, Victoria was swept to safety by Andrew Hammond. The older man's ranch

near Cheyenne became her sanctuary, or at least seemed
so until her drunken savior ravaged her one storm-swept
night.

Sober, in the sunshine, Andrew had apologized, and
within a year they had wed, she sixteen, he forty-six. She
had come to admire his strength and ruthlessness, and
continued success in a hard business. Living well made
up for her husband's boorishness, when drink took over,
and she had a grudging affection for the sober version of
him in the early years. Three boys came of their alter-
nately tender and violent marital bed.

Should she have believed the disgruntled, fired ranch
ramrod who between the sheets shared secrets perhaps
better kept? That Andrew had swindled and stolen far
more money from her late father than had San Francisco's venal city hall? That her boys' father had sold her
own father out to the vigilantes and handed him over to
them for their necktie party? And that her mother's suicide had been less about the loss of a husband and their
fortune, and more about being rejected after years as
Hammond's secret lover?

Skepticism would have been the better part of valor,
but she knew the truth the ramrod's words suggested. She
stayed with Andrew, never a mention of any of this passing between them, and she went on sharing his bed, in
both his sober and inebriated states. She did this for
many years, until on another stormy night—one that recalled the nightmare of her deflowering—she'd had
enough of his drunken debauchery.

She had sat naked by his bedside with a Colt .45 in
hand, waiting for him to stir, waiting for him to wake,
and when he did, she fired a bullet into his belly. She did
this knowing full well the placement of her gunshot
would mean he'd take a good while to die.

When her oldest boy, Hugh, sixteen, ran into the room and saw what she had done, and stood open-mouthed while his father bubbled blood, the youth put an arm around his mother's shoulder.

"We'll make up a story," he said.

His father had often beaten the spunky, wiseacre boy, for cause (sober), and for sport (drunk).

Hugh said, "We'll say a thief broke in."

"No," she said.

"No?"

"Someone with a grudge."

"Yes! But there are so many. . . ."

"This will be a stranger. One we heard shout, 'At last my indignities are avenged!' "

Having witnessed this exchange, eyes wide, mouth filled with frothing red, Andrew Hammond died seconds later, his hands clasped over his wound and blood oozing between his fingers. But the oozing soon stopped, as dead men do not bleed.

Mother and son worked up a story, and created the impression of a break-in, and of course a description of no real person, and spread some money behind the scenes. With the ranch now hers, rumors swirled. She built the spread up over the next few years, sold out, and moved to Colorado, near the New Mexico Territory, toward new opportunities, and away from the talk.

The hard winter of the Big Die-Up had inspired this southward move, where opportunities for investing in cattle land were one benefit of the otherwise disastrous blizzards.

A knock at the library door interrupted her reverie.

"Yes?"

Byers stuck his head in. "Mr. Colman is waiting on the west veranda, ma'am."

"Good. Tell him I'll be a few minutes. Have Conchita bring him a coffee with whiskey. Remind her he likes more of the latter than the former."

Victoria went to her bedroom and got out of her mourning gown with its mantilla and slipped into black crepe, not for grieving, rather a dress with gaucho-style pantaloons and a scooped bodice, its jacket decorated with white filigree trim. She added a silver necklace, then allowed two plump tendrils of her black curls to fall to her shoulders. She did this only in certain situations, as hair as long as hers worn down was the way of saloon wantons. So was make-up, but she paused at her mirror to apply just enough for her purposes.

Black leather boots were the last touch, fit for riding.

On the veranda, at a wicker table in a wicker chair, her ramrod, Clay Colman, sat sipping his coffee and looking out at the stand of tall firs edging the shallow backyard, its grass well-tended in the modern manner. Hearing her footfall, he stood quickly and turned to her, hat in hand.

He was a handsome devil of perhaps thirty-five, blond, blue-eyed, clean-shaven, sharp-featured, in a brown leather vest over a brown-and-green plaid shirt, his pants canvas, his Boss of the Plains hat dark brown and sporting a rattlesnake band.

The hatband was a vestige, a symbol, of his having ridden with the criminal gang in Arizona known as the Cowboys. This was not a drawback—as a long experienced rustler, her ramrod knew his way around cattle. And the future of the Circle G depended on raiding below the border for fresh stock.

"You wear black well . . . Miz Hammond," he said. His voice was slow, like melting butter. Yet there was always something at least a little salty in the way he spit his words out. Maybe that came from the cocky bastard knowing how handsome he was. Of course, she was well aware of her own beauty. With her money, that put her one up on him.

She gestured to the wicker table and he pulled a chair out for her and she sat, then he sat opposite.

"I don't waste time in mourning," she said. "I leave lamentation to my lessers."

Showing her broken heart to anyone, she felt, was beneath her. If a woman wanted to be strong in the West— if she wanted to be strong *anywhere*—she could not so indulge herself.

"No, Miz, you go straight to revenge," he said, and there was a wolfishness about the way half his upper lip curled as he spoke the words. "The way a *man* would."

Her shrug was barely noticeable. "Revenge will come in time. William's murder is not our major concern at the moment."

"It's not?"

She shook her head. "It was William's own frailty that led to his ruin. I won't pretend with you, Clay, that I'm not aware of that. Of my son putting himself in that position." Her rage bubbled but she contained it. "The point is this—Caleb York disrespected me, disrespected all of us at the Circle G, by handling William's bad judgment in so . . . *final* a way."

Colman was outright sneering now, and lifting a vein-roped fist, shaking it. "That son of a bitch York. . . . Wearing a badge don't make him any less a killer."

She frowned in interest. "You have a history with our famous sheriff?"

Colman let the fist become fingers and pawed the air. "Not that he'd ever know. But he took the lives of more than one good man I rode with. Back when he was working for Wells Fargo."

"Ah."

The ramrod sat forward, knitting improbably dark eyebrows in the midst of all that blondness. "You know how it says on them posters, 'Wanted Dead or Alive'? I don't know of him *ever* bringing a man back alive." He grunted. "Dead was easier than watching a prisoner on the ride back and feedin' him and sleepin' round a campfire with some poor bastard angling to light out."

Her eyebrows lifted. "York may not be the man he once was."

Colman blinked. "How's that, Miz Hammond?"

"I spoke to him today. Our famous sheriff came around with his tail tucked between his legs. Humble and sorry about what he had to do. Dripping with pity for the poor mother of his victim."

Colman frowned as he shook his head. "Don't sound like Caleb York. Don't sound like him a'tall."

"He's older. He's seen more. And this gives us . . ." By which she meant *me*. ". . . an unexpected advantage."

"How so, Miz Hammond?"

She folded her arms, crossed her legs. "York will be more sympathetically inclined toward me and my thinking than he otherwise might have been." She cocked her head. "Have you ever seen the Cullen girl?"

He nodded. "In town. Never spoke to her. No cause to. Pretty young thing, though. But hard to imagine she's up to running a ranch—*any* ranch, let alone a spread the size of the Bar-O."

Victoria's eyes narrowed. "She grew up on that ranch. I have it on reliable authority that she has a good head on those slim shoulders of hers, supported by a spine inherited from her late father. And the late George Cullen is rather beloved in these parts."

He snorted. "I heard he was just a blind old coot."

"Cullen established Trinidad. Practically . . . *invented* it. He brought in shopkeepers and a banker and a doctor and more, just for the personal convenience of having a town nearby. When the way you buy supplies is to set somebody up in the supply *business*, well . . . you may have wound up a dead blind old coot, but you were a living, breathing man once. The kind of man who built this country."

"Like your late husband."

"Like my late husband," she said, and she meant it, though she would gladly kill that monster again a hundred times over.

As for Claymore Colman, he was the third ramrod since the disgruntled ex-foreman who had, in bed, told her the truth about Andrew Hammond. She had a habit, or perhaps it was a policy, of getting close to her ramrods. Of having a man she could depend upon—*not* lean on—who could bring a strong hand to the cow herders, and give them someone to look up to and even fear . . . since some of them would never learn to respect a woman boss, even when she literally wore the pants.

"You play poker," she said to him.

"I do."

"Have you ever gone into a game that you knew would last a while? Where players with bankrolls had come from far and wide, and the intention was to play through the night? Perhaps even to play till one winner was left standing? Or perhaps I should say sitting."

"I have."

"So a game like that has to be played one round at a time, carefully, skillfully, strategically. You have to read the other players. You have to know how they think. You have to know their 'tells.' "

He grinned. "Miz Hammond . . . you never played poker in your life."

"Oh but I did. In my father's saloon on the Barbary Coast. He taught me well. He would bring me into a game when I was, oh, thirteen, fourteen? And some of the men would howl with laughter, and others would just howl, but it was my father's joint and if they wanted to play, it was house rules. You know about house rules, Clay?"

"I do."

"So it was a novelty, having a child playing poker in a den of iniquity. Just a young lass fiddling with those colored chips, merely another game like hopscotch or marbles. *Only I would win.* Win big. And the funny thing, Clay? Those men almost always loved it. Of course, I was a pretty thing. Charming. Innocent."

"I bet you were." He emphasized "were" perhaps a little too much for her liking.

"My point is," Victoria said, "we will deal with Caleb York later. After he's ceased to be of use to us."

To me.

Colman asked, "How will he be of use to us?"

Victoria rose, curled a finger at him to follow her. They stood at the edge of the veranda by a low-slung white rail.

She spoke softly now. Not that she thought someone might overhear, but . . . still, she spoke softly. "You say you saw Willa Cullen in town? Did you ask around about her?"

"A little."

They were standing close.

She asked, "What did you learn?"

"Cullen gal and York are friendly. Of course, he's

friendly with that fancy woman that runs the Victory, too." He shook his head. "I don't get what they see in him."

She did.

Victoria said, "I've already asked Caleb to speak to Willa Cullen on my behalf."

" 'Caleb,' is it? Will he do that?"

She nodded confidently. "I believe so. At least he'll tell her about my hope to buy her spread, and that should at least cause sparks. Willa Cullen may not like having her . . . beau . . . delivering a message from . . ."

"Another woman?"

She laughed a little. "Yes. And should he be successful in getting Miss Cullen to meet with me, and encourage her to hear my offer for the Bar-O? She might not then be so grateful to her precious Caleb York. Because I doubt she will appreciate the modest price I'm prepared to pay."

"Because of Sugar Creek."

"Because of Sugar Creek." She smiled toward the trees. "The only stream from the Purgatory River that hasn't been fouled by cattle dying in it. And I include the Purgatory itself."

She could smell the stream from here. Fresh. Unspoiled.

The ramrod nodded toward those trees. "We're already camped there. You know that. Ready to defend your property."

"Yes, and your efforts are satisfactory thus far. But with a man like York around, we need some insurance. I know you've assembled some of your . . . compatriots from the old Arizona days. But rustlers . . . forgive my frankness . . . rustlers who can handle a firearm are not enough. Caleb York—you said it yourself—is a killer."

"He's that," Colman admitted.

Her laugh was rueful. "They're already writing dime novels about his 'exploits' in Trinidad. How he gunned down Harry Gauge, the crooked sheriff whose ranch this once was. How he massacred the Rhomer boys in the street, and sent the Preacherman to hell, and that ghost town with the hotel for outlaws? He shut it down and left nobody or anything standing. He's a one-man army."

Colman seemed to be working at being unimpressed. "Well, he does have a deputy."

She laughed once. "My understanding is his deputy's an old rummy."

"An old rummy with a hair-trigger temper and the same kind of finger on a scattergun." He looked at her with a nasty smile. "But even the great Caleb York lets his guard down now and again. They killed Wild Bill, didn't they?"

"Oh, and how did you and your friends do with Wyatt Earp?"

His chin jutted. "His brother Morgan bought it."

"Virgil Earp's still a lawman, I understand. And Wyatt himself is alive and well. Now, now . . . I don't mean to be hard on you, Claymore. You're a good boy. A good man. But I would feel more secure if you took on some *really* bad men. Bravos, we called them in San Francisco. I mean outright shootists."

He nodded. "Pistoleros can be found."

She raised a hard, tiny fist. "Yes, yes, any one of whom could likely handle York head-on, or at least from ambush . . . but ambushes can fail, and we need more than one ace in our poker hand, don't we? To bet with confidence?"

He frowned, almost as if he were holding back tears.

"I can take him out, Miz Hammond. You can leave it to me. I could do it right *now*! Today!"

She held up a hand. "I know. I know. But this is a game that's going to go for a while, remember? Into the night and on to the next day and . . . who can say? For now I want to see how thoroughly I can get Caleb York to do my bidding, as he tries to make up for the tragedy he visited upon me. Only when I have wrung every last drop of guilt and usefulness from him will I turn to you . . . my loyal ramrod . . . my strong, hard man . . . to take him out. To rid the world of the pestilence that is Caleb York."

"Damn right," he said.

"Then I'll use my new influence in the county to put a sheriff in office who I can really control."

He grinned. "Bought and paid for. The best kind."

She was almost whispering. "Now. Here's what I want you to do. Go to Las Vegas and find me some thoroughly reprehensible but highly skilled hired guns."

"Happy to."

Her lips neared his ear. "And tonight . . . well, why don't you sleep in the guest room tonight?"

"Not on the banks by Sugar Creek with my boys?"

She shook her head and the thick hanging curls came along for the ride. "No. Your *segundo*, Luis, will come fetch you if you're needed. The game is in early rounds yet, so nothing will likely happen. But, tonight, in your bed, see if you can come up with three ways to kill Caleb York. Three plans that you feel confident in executing. And bring them to me. And we'll talk them over."

"First thing tomorrow?"

She was looking right at him now; the firs seemed to be leaning a little, trying to hear. "No, no. Must I spell it out? Midnight?"

Byers and the help slept in the west wing of the house, and Victoria slept in the east wing. The guest room was just down the hall from her. The ramrod knew the way, but also knew he had to wait to be invited.

"Midnight . . . Victoria," he said.

She rested a hand on his shoulder. "Three ways to kill Caleb York. Think of them as . . . sweet nothings."

CHAPTER FIVE

The day after he and Willa Cullen enjoyed a wonderful afternoon together that had ended at an unfortunate impasse, Caleb York strolled into the hotel dining room, where he hung his hat on a wall peg and glanced around.

He'd been asked to meet with his friend and business partner, Raymond L. Parker, and Trinidad's mayor, Jasper P. Hardy. They had requested the confab for what purpose York did not know. But the sheriff was first to arrive.

The dining room at the Trinidad House Hotel, where York kept a room at the city's expense, had its usual noontime crowd of shop owners, businessmen traveling through, and a rancher or two. Clerks and other hired workers dined at the café, while ranch hands in town for whatever reason often partook of the Victory Saloon's free lunch, where an array of salted items kept them thirsty. The hotel dining room's patronage, on the other hand, was as close to elite as this town of three hundred or so in the middle of nowhere could manage.

While York did not regard himself as one of the prosperous class, he did view himself as a professional man.

His black coat and trousers and string tie represented the unofficial uniform. Still, even after all these months, he did not feel at home in the Trinidad House dining room, with its dark wood, fancy chairs, linen tablecloths, fine place settings, and cut-glass chandeliers.

Nonetheless, he selected his regular table by the window. He told himself this was to enable him to keep an eye on things on the street; but he also meant to be seen by the successful men who dined here regularly. Since he'd had the surprise—a pleasant one, but a surprise just the same—of being handsomely remembered in George Cullen's will, Caleb York had come to see Trinidad as more than just a bump in the road he'd stumbled over last year.

His sheriff post had been thrust upon him, after he somewhat inadvertently "cleaned up the town" of crooked Sheriff Harry Gauge and his bunch. In the process he'd got his head turned by Willa Cullen, and York and her father George became cronies. Suddenly the detective job waiting for him in San Diego with the Pinkertons seemed to recede in the distance, as if he were perhaps riding off in the wrong direction.

York had insisted that he was only filling the sheriff slot temporarily, but the town fathers had kept throwing money and perquisites at him. The Citizens Committee, who he worked for, seemed to view as a boon to the community the very reputation as a gunfighter that York himself considered a burden.

Coffee was delivered to him automatically, and he sipped the wonderful stuff—any opportunity to sample something other than the bilge his deputy concocted was seized upon. Shortly, Raymond Parker breezed through the handsome lobby into this impressive dining room in what was otherwise a very average hotel.

The tall, white-haired, white-mustached banker, in his early fifties, wore his prosperity as casually and confidently as York did his .44 (not strapped down at the moment, its holstered nose pointed at the parquet floor). Parker's double-breasted gray trimmed-black Newmarket coat, lighter gray waistcoat, and darker gray trousers were set off by the almost absurdly Western touch of a broad-brimmed gray Stetson.

But Parker had a right to wear that hat. No Eastern dude, he had been George Cullen's partner—they had established the Bar-O together—and sold out due to problems with their late third partner, Burt O'Malley, the "O" in Bar-O. Parker had yearned for the big city anyway, and the money he took out of the ranch soon found its way into budding businesses all across the Southwest. Today the man owned restaurants, hotels, and several banks, including Trinidad's.

York rose. The two men shook hands, exchanged smiles and greetings. Parker had been in town a little over a week, but this was the first time the two had sat down together.

"The mayor will join us," Parker said, "in a quarter of an hour. I thought, beforehand, it would be best if you and I took a few minutes alone."

A waiter in black livery and an apron arrived just then and York told him to return when the third member of their party arrived.

York eyed his friend with care. "Raymond, is there a problem? With construction, perhaps?"

The banker's smile was knowing. "No. Not in any major way. The winter has postponed things a bit, is all."

He lighted up a plump cigar with a safety match, then waved it out. That was no nickel smoke, either—one of those Cubans that set you back two bits.

Parker went on: "The land is too damn soggy for proper building to begin—not a typical problem in this part of the world. But construction will start soon."

"Good."

George Cullen had left York half an acre of land at the east end of town, to the rear of the livery stable. Cullen had apparently left York the bequest out of appreciation for the stranger's town taming. And perhaps also to encourage him to stay around Trinidad and marry daughter Willa.

Now Parker was funding a train station on that parcel, with a spur between Trinidad and Las Vegas, New Mexico, coming courtesy of the Santa Fe Railroad.

Parker leaned forward; he kept his voice down. "What I want to discuss, Caleb, briefly . . . is your options."

"I'm listening," York said.

The banker gestured with the cigar between his fingers. "You're in an enviable position, my friend. I needn't remind you that we are equal partners who will be receiving handsome monthly fees from both the Santa Fe and the city of Trinidad. And among your options . . . if I may delicately tread into your personal business . . ."

"Can I stop you?"

"You can. I do not mean to intrude in your . . . affairs."

York didn't like the sound of that, but he said, "Go on."

"One option is to bolster that young woman of yours in rebuilding her father's ranching business. You'll have money to help her, after all." He poked the air with the cigar. "You told me once that you came from farming stock, but also that you'd sooner be dead than plow. But you could plow money into her spread, and help run the place, without fixing a fence post or punching a cow or digging up a turnip out of the ground, for that matter."

"Turn in my badge and gun for a ledger book."

Parker tossed a hand in the air. "Frankly, yes. You'll be in a position to invest in businesses here in town, and you'll want to keep an eye on them. You'll learn about every one of them and soon be advising the proprietors as to what they're buying and what they're selling."

"Sounds like a dream. The kind you wake up from in a cold sweat."

Parker shrugged. "Or . . . you can hang onto that badge and gun. I happen to know the mayor will be trying to convince you of doing just that. Now, times are changing. There's no doubt of that. And in some respects, the Wild West will soon exist only in memory and in Buffalo Bill Cody's circus."

"Which is why," York reminded the banker, "I was on my way to San Diego."

"A big modern city, yes, where your detective skills would be needed no matter what changes God and Man might visit upon us. But you, Caleb, are in a unique situation."

"Am I." He had the distinct feeling he was being sold something—snake oil perhaps—though he wasn't sure just what that something might be. But Parker had never been one to take advantage—even giving advice came rare from the man.

"In the next few years," Parker said, glancing out the window between hazy curtains at a dusty street, "this town will be inundated not only with new business but the old businesses that come with it: saloons, brothels, thieving, killing. The Victory will have rivals, and Miss Rita Filley's good efforts to drive prostitution out from under her roof will come up against the efforts of far less scrupulous entrepreneurs. Men with guns and badges will most definitely still be needed."

"That's more of the same, not changin' times."

Parker raised a palm, as if balancing some invisible object. "Times will change for the better and for the worse, Caleb. If you stay a lawman, in a town that booms, you'll be more of a police chief than a sheriff or marshal, whatever term they may hang on you. And you'll have a staff consisting of far more than the redoubtable Deputy Tulley."

The waiter came over and refilled their coffee cups.

York drank from his. "If I am to keep at the lawing, Raymond, I mean to make of it a profession—like a doctor, a lawyer."

"And well you should. After all, think of the business you bring to both!" A grin bristled the white mustache. "Caleb, I have no opinion in this other than a desire for what's best for my business partner . . . my friend."

"I appreciate that."

Again the banker shrugged. "You will soon be a man of means. If you choose to join that sweet girl on her ranch with her dream of making her dead father happy, God bless you. If you choose to retire from enforcing the law and lean back and count the money coming in, there's no shame in that either—it will bring its own responsibilities."

Now Parker leaned in, eyes narrowing shrewdly.

"But if you *stay* a lawman, Caleb, in this part of the country? You may be able to practice your profession and even manage not to get killed doing it."

"Doesn't that sound promising."

"You'll have a staff of your own experienced men, probably in blue uniforms with nightsticks, to take the chances for you. You can sit at your desk. You can ride in parades and cut the ribbons on businesses, as the famous Southwestern lawman who helped tame the West."

York frowned. "A tourist attraction."

"Yes, and why not? It would be a small but important part of who you are. Who you'll be. Bill Cody goes around playing himself in a show. That's fine for him—he was always something of a fraud anyway. But Caleb York? People can point to him and say, 'That's him! That's the legend!' "

"Do you really think I care about that?"

Parker shook his head soundly. "No. In New Orleans they call it a lagniappe. It's just something you bring along, something extra—the way those who hire you throw in perquisites."

In the double doorway between the lobby and the dining room, the mayor of Trinidad appeared. Jasper Hardy was also the town barber and York suspected the man's good grooming had encouraged his appointment by the Citizens Committee—elections weren't being held yet in Trinidad.

The mayor, perhaps forty, was small and slight but dignified in his gray frock coat, his black slicked-back hair and elaborate handlebar mustache a splendid advertisement for his tonsorial parlor. He hung up his derby on a wall peg and paused to nod at the rest of his already seated party at the table by the window.

They nodded back, and the mayor sat next to the banker. The waiter materialized and took their order—everyone had oyster stew, the specialty of the house.

"I have something for you, Sheriff," the mayor said in his reedy tenor, "which I hope will please you. Which I hope you will accept."

Parker was watching the barber with faint amusement; clearly he knew what was coming.

Hardy dipped his hand into a coat pocket and placed what he'd withdrawn on the linen tablecloth, near York—a shield-type badge.

"Thank you, Your Honor," York said, tapping the tin star on his gray shirt, "but what I have will do."

"I'm not suggesting a trade," the mayor said, a lilt in his already high voice. "This is an addition."

A lagniappe?

The mayor was saying, "You need not wear it, or you may choose to instead . . . swap them out, depending on the occasion. The situation."

Parker's amusement had faded. "Let's not be coy, Jasper. Tell Caleb what you have in mind. Share what it is that you have in mind for him."

The little mayor folded his hands. "As you may know, I have a certain . . . influence with the Territorial government in Santa Fe."

Parker said to York, "Jasper's sister is married to the governor's brother."

York grinned at this revelation, which had somehow been kept from him. He'd often wondered how it was the undersized barber had come to hold the political reins in Trinidad. It couldn't be good grooming entirely.

"Our Citizens Committee," the mayor said, "will henceforth be known as the City Council. I have been appointed mayor for a five-year term, after which we will have our first elections."

That was a savvy play for both the mayor and the governor—Trinidad would have its growth spurt in the next five years. Fortunes could be made. A little man could be a king, at least for five years.

"That badge," the mayor said, pointing to the silver shield, "identifies you as marshal of Trinidad."

Indeed it was engraved MARSHAL.

"I prefer," Caleb said, openly skeptical, "being county sheriff."

With the tax collecting, it paid better.

"You will still be sheriff, with a five-year term like mine," Hardy said, his smile lifting the elaborate mustache, like curtains rising. "With a second paycheck, equal to the one you're already receiving, and will continue to receive."

York squinted suspiciously at the diminutive politician. "What new responsibilities does this entail?"

The mayor shrugged. "None. It's the same job you've been doing. Of course, as Trinidad grows with the spur, and becomes a railhead for cattle—surely that industry will rebound, at least to a respectable degree—the scope of your responsibilities will grow."

That small army of men in blue with nightsticks of Parker's marched into York's mind. "I would need more staff."

"Certainly. Deputy Tulley has exceeded all of our expectations, but you will need good men. Officers. I assure you that the City Council will approve reasonable requests for additional personnel."

Their oyster stew arrived.

They ate in relative silence, with occasional chitchat ensuing, but between the mayor and the banker only. York just put the food away at an easy pace, but his mind was galloping. The badge caught light from the high noon sun, glinting, winking, like the facets of a cut diamond.

When their plates had been cleared, and the coffee cups refilled, York said, "I would want Tulley's salary doubled, as well."

"Done," the mayor said. "And then there's the matter

of the house here in town, construction of which was already under way when the blizzards struck."

"The use of which is mine while I'm in office."

Hardy shook his head. "No, Sheriff. It will be yours free and clear. The deed will be signed over to you. We ask only one thing."

"And what is that?"

"No further talk from you of San Diego and the Pinks. You will sign a contract and make a commitment to Trinidad." The mayor pushed away from the table. "Well, I have to get back to my customers. Time and tonsorial needs wait for no man." He stood—not tall, but stood. "May I leave the badge?"

York nodded.

The mayor rushed over for his hat and went quickly out, leaving no time for the expression of second thoughts.

Parker finished his coffee. His cigar had long since gone out and resided rather sadly in a Trinidad House glass ash tray.

"Well," the banker said. "You seem to have selected your option."

"I seem to."

"No doubt Miss Cullen will be pleased. She's gone to some lengths to keep you away from that position with the Pinkertons in San Diego." The mayor pushed away and rose. "Now, if you'll excuse me, I have some legal matters to discuss with Mr. Curtis."

Arlen Curtis was the attorney who represented both York and Parker in the various train station dealings.

"Give him my regards," York said reflexively.

The banker nodded, signed the check to his room, and left.

A few minutes later, shaded by wooden awnings, York was heading up the boardwalk to the jailhouse. The street no longer wore its usual layer of sand, brought in from the nearby Purgatory River, to keep the dust down; the snow had swallowed up, and carried off, much of that sand, and the damp ground it left behind turned hard and rutted, not yet given to dust.

A handful of women in gingham and calico were out strolling along shopping, and men in work attire whether farm or town were occasionally going in and coming out of businesses. This small-town world—with its hardware store, apothecary, mercantile store, bank, telegraph office, saddle shop, and single saloon—had been easy enough to supervise where keeping the peace went. But as Trinidad grew, so would his obligations.

Of course, so would his paycheck—*paychecks*—and his staff would consist of more than one eccentric, re-formed desert rat. He shouldn't look a gift horse in the mouth, not that he was inclined to look any horse in the mouth. Something was unsettling him, though.

Maybe it was just change.

And change was coming. It was something you couldn't ride around, and you couldn't jump over it, either. Maybe . . . maybe . . . you could tame it, the way the right lawman could an unruly town.

Someone was sitting on the bench out front of the jail—Bill Jackson, the cowhand born a Mississippi slave who Willa hired on as her foreman. York had spoken to him a few times, just in passing, and knew he had a reputation among his men as hard but fair.

Jackson got to his feet as York approached, and doffed his sombrero. He was near tall as York, his hair cropped short, his features finely carved, set off by a horseshoe mustache; he wore a faded blue army shirt, a bright red-

and-white bandanna knotted at his neck, chaps over denim pants, boots with spurs, and a waist-slung bandolier with a .38 Colt Lightning revolver.

Holding his sombrero in both hands, a frowning Jackson asked, "Might I have a word, sir?" It was "suh," as the black man had brought his Mississippi accent along when he came West.

"Certainly, Mr. Jackson. Have you a problem?"

Dark eyes in deep sockets went tight. "It's Miz Cullen has the problem. They's some rough fellers gathered at Sugar Creek. They is heeled to the hilt, Sheriff."

"The creek runs through Circle G land."

"That it does. But they's always been an understandin' that the river and the creek was fair game for any herd."

"That was the understanding with the *previous* owners."

Jackson nodded, but his frown remained. "That understandin' went two ways. If the creek was dry any given year, they was welcome to water their cows in the Purgatory, where it run through Bar-O range."

"Right. But the creek isn't dry this year. And the Purgatory's fouled."

Jackson let out a grunt of a sigh. "Nobody knows that better than I, Sheriff. We've maybe a third of our boys draggin' dead stinkin' steers outta that river. Pilin' 'em, burnin' 'em. Jobs don't come much worse. We're doin' our best to clear the Purg, and by next season those waters should be runnin' nice and clean and clear again. But that's a long ways off."

York pushed his hat back. "That understanding you spoke of, Mr. Jackson—as far as I know, there's nothing on paper. I would like to help, but the law seems to be with Victoria Hammond."

Eyebrows rose. "A thing like this can get out of hand, Sheriff. I was in the thick of things down Lincoln County way, some while back. Shootin' lasted for years and many a life was lost."

The Lincoln County War between rival cattle barons raged from '78 through '81. Among other things, it had made a name for both Billy the Kid and Pat Garrett.

"The best solution," York said, "is for Miss Cullen and Mrs. Hammond to come to mutually agreeable terms."

Hell, York thought. *I'm already sounding like a citified official.*

Jackson said acidly, "The only terms that female hell spawn might agree to is Miz Cullen sellin' out. Sheriff . . . you and Miz Cullen have friendly relations."

York decided the man meant nothing scurrilous about that.

The foreman's earnestness was almost painful to hear. "Could you tell the Hammond woman that if her rough boys go shootin' freely at the Cullen cowhands . . . or shoot their steers if they start to watering 'em . . . that you'll throw their backsides behind bars?" He jerked a thumb at the jailhouse. "Or send them straight to hell, with that storied pistol of yorn, which is fine with me."

"I thought you wanted to avoid trouble. Or are you just fine with *me* having trouble?"

"Meaning no disrespect, it's what you're paid for, Sheriff. These ain't cowpunchers of the normal variety. These is that rabble what wears the rattlesnake hatband."

The riffraff remainder of the Arizona rustlers, the Cowboys.

Jackson was frowning again, desperation coming into his voice . . . and an edge. "*Talk sense* with that witch out to the Circle G, Sheriff. Elseways, I will have to enlist gunhands myself to match them bastards bullet for bullet."

York raised a cautionary palm. "Easy now, Mr. Jackson. This jail can hold all sorts."

"Oh, we won't draw first blood, Sheriff. We won't have to." He slammed the sombrero on. It drooped in front, from being tugged to keep out the sun riding herd. "I hoped you was good enough friends with Miz Cullen to try and head this thing off. Don't look that way."

And the foreman strode off, steaming, spurs jangling.

CHAPTER SIX

Several days later, two sessions of highly unusual job interviews were held in the same meeting room at the rear of the Imperial Saloon in Las Vegas, New Mexico. Unbeknownst to the two men considering candidates for their respective female boss's employ, the first session was conducted at ten in the morning, the other at two in the afternoon, for the convenience of their host, Vicente Silva.

In Las Vegas, pop. 4000, men desiring entertainment in the form of gambling, drinking, and painted ladies had numerous choices; but the Imperial on the plaza limited itself to the first two of those options—men desiring loose women would have to look elsewhere.

Owner Silva was, after all, a well-respected, upright entrepreneur who gave to his church and to charity, and a gracious, impressive presence at the Imperial. His attire impeccable, his beard well trimmed, this handsome, mannerly, intelligent man welcomed silver and copper miners, cattle and sheep ranchers, beef and wool buyers, merchants, and bankers to the most popular drinking establishment in San Miguel County.

From the endless mahogany bar in the saloon itself to the second-floor casino, the Imperial was both well appointed and accommodating, the tall, solidly built host as affable as he was prosperous. What the respectable citizens of Las Vegas did not know (but which certain less respectable ones did) was that Silva was the head of the Forty Bandits, who specialized in murder, thievery, and rustling, as well as driving out settlers through arson, violence, and fence cutting, in an effort to restore common pastures.

But even members of his gang were unaware that their imposing boss had been a criminal since he was twenty; that back in Wyoming, he had run off with a railroad laborer's wife, leaving in his wake her murdered husband, buried with chest slashed and head cut off.

So Silva was neither offended nor surprised when Clay Colman ambled into the Imperial to ask the proprietor if he could spare some top gunhands from the White Caps, as Silva's gang was also known—men with nerve and killing ways.

Colman had ridden with the Bandits himself for a while, a few years back. Now the sometime rustler was ramrod at the Circle G, which was honest work of a sort, keeping in mind the dishonest reputation of the new owner, the widow Hammond, said to be as beautiful as she was relentless.

The two men stood at one end of the bar with no one—not even the bartender who'd served the blond cowboy a beer—within earshot.

His silver-rattlesnake-banded black hat pushed back cockily on his head, Colman said, "Miz Hammond will pay top dollar."

"Spell it out."

"Twenty-five a week." He paused for a gulp of beer. Swallowed, and said, "Bonus money if things get dicey."

Twenty-five a month was decent cowboy money. Forty, if the kind of work the Bandits did was involved.

Silva asked, seeming unimpressed, "How long?"

"One month's work anyways, Mr. Silva. More maybe, but not less."

"Ten percent of each man's pay," Silva said. "On top of that twenty-five. First month's worth in advance."

Colman shrugged. "Fair enough."

Silva would take another ten from the men, as well; but Colman didn't need to know that.

The ramrod raised a forefinger. "I'll want to talk to each, Mr. Silva. Size 'em up."

"My opinion's not good enough for you, Clay?"

He grinned. "Your opinion's what makes 'em worth considerin'. But I don't buy a horse without a look at the teeth."

"So then you want candidates. Prospects."

"I want guns, Mr. Silva. I want bad men I can trust."

Silva smiled, not broadly but meaningfully. "A scarce commodity. But I can deliver. Take a room at the Plaza Hotel. I'll have applicants for you here at ten tomorrow morning."

Not long after Clay Colman had gone out, another familiar face from the past presented itself, that of a striking black cowpoke in an oversize sombrero, its brim pushed up in front. The newcomer came directly over to where Silva was still at the unpopulated end of the bar. The cowboy offered his hand and the two men shook.

Silva had tried to enlist Bill Jackson for the Bandits several years ago and got nowhere—this was a tough, skilled cattleman, hampered by an honest streak.

"Nice to see you, Bill," Silva said. "That job offer is still open, if that's what brings you by."

"Thank you, no, señor," the black cowhand said. "I'm foreman down at the Bar-O now."

Two Trinidad ramrods in one afternoon?

"Reason I'm here," Jackson said, "is to line up some pistoleros. Three, maybe four."

And all at once it made sense to Silva—he'd got word that the Hammond woman was buying up smaller spreads south of Las Vegas, and naturally she would turn her greedy eyes on the Cullen place. Perhaps a cattle war was brewing, although Colman had spoken of something short term.

Wishful thinking?

Silva ordered up a beer for Jackson, nothing for himself.

"I might be able to spare some talent from my stable," Silva said, as Jackson sipped the cold brew. "For the right price."

"Cullen gal pays good," Jackson said. "She's got her late daddy's blood runnin' in her. You name a fair rate and she'll bite."

"A hundred a month, plus ten percent surcharge for my trouble."

Jackson's eyebrows went up. "Might be more than a month."

"Twenty-five a week's the rate, hundred-dollar minimum. You want me to pick 'em?"

"Meanin' no offense, Mr. Silva, I'd like a look at the cut of their jib myself. Like to talk to each man on his lonesome."

"You don't find shootists among the Sunday school crowd."

"I know. Make 'em hard, but men I can trust."

"You may depend on it." Silva gestured toward the street. "Galinas Hotel over in the settlement takes your kind, Mr. Jackson. Be here tomorrow afternoon, 2 p.m. I'll have potential recruits available."

The meeting room at the rear of the Imperial Saloon was, unlike the saloon itself and its gambling rooms, nothing fancy. Banquet tables were pushed back against the walls and, in the middle of the otherwise naked room, a wooden card table with one chair, facing the door, had been provided for the interview process.

Colman took the chair.

Silva sent in a man Colman recognized.

Dave Carson was of average size, a little bigger than most cowboys, a breed that ran runty, since ranchers hired on smaller hands to make it easier on the horses.

Carson stood on the other side of the card table. He wore a nice if frayed dark suit with a vest and no tie with a collarless shirt, his pale yellow hat worn with the brim up. His eyes were dark and close-set and he wore a mustache on an otherwise boyish face. A Colt revolver rode high on his right hip—looked like a Thunderer .41 to Colman.

Dave took off his hat and smiled shyly. "How you been, Colman? Hear you're ramrod down Circle G way."

"I am."

"And Mr. Silva says you're hirin'. But I ain't that big on cowboyin' no more."

"Not lookin' for that. I got plenty of cowpunchers. I need fellas handy with a six-gun. Boys not fearful of bullets flyin' in either direction."

Dave made a face and shrugged. "I kilt four one night."

"In one night? Do tell."

The boyish killer nodded. "I was a deputy marshal in Dodge at the time. Dance hall there, some of the Henry cowpokes was scarin' the women and roughin' up the men. I come in with my boss and one of them Henry boys shot the marshal, dead as yesterday. I start in shootin' them. Didn't last long. But the town fired me. Wouldn't you know it?"

"Why did they fire you?"

He made another face. "One of the four I kilt weren't one of the Henry boys. Just some fool who ran for the back door when the shootin' started and I miscalculated."

Colman made a click in his cheek. "You musta felt bad about that."

"Not really. Honest mistake." Dave cleared his throat to announce changing the subject. "Who do you have needs killin', Clay?"

"A war's brewing near Trinidad. Two ranchers fighting over water. Does it matter to you who's in the right?"

"Doesn't not matter." He shrugged. "But I ain't particular, if the dimes stack up."

"How many you killed in your time, Dave?"

He frowned, thinking. "Does Mexicans count?"

Colman grinned. "Better not let ol' Silva hear you say that."

Dave grinned; it was an awkward, yellow thing. "Oh, he ain't touchy about such things, nor is I. Most of the White Caps is Mexican and they's as good a men as most. It's just when you're calculatin' kills, there is some folks don't count Mexicans. Or Indians."

"They count when they're comin' at you with guns or knives." He shifted in the hard chair. "Dave, let me fill you in on the particulars."

"Oh, like I said, I ain't particular."

"No, I mean . . . you've got the job, if the money sounds right to you."

"Money don't never sound wrong."

Dave was the first man Colman hired.

Billy Bassett was maybe ten years older than Dave Carson, a skinny character with a full mustache that looked like it might weigh near as much as he did. He wore a battered canvas jacket over a gray twill shirt, chaps over denims, and a low-slung Remington revolver. By way of introduction, he told a story of an encounter in a saloon not as posh as the Imperial.

"I have killed my share," he told Colman in a low drawl. "Maybe the one people talk about is when the four brothers of a man named Drew come to Wichita lookin' for me. But I found them first."

"Is that the time you just stepped through the Long Branch doors and just started shooting?"

Billy snapped his fingers. "That's the one! Two died on the spot. Two others died later that night from me shootin' 'em earlier. Hell, I was gone afore the smoke cleared. And I killed nary an innocent bystander, not that many in that particular drinkin' hole was what you might call innocent."

No bystanders. Billy had one up on Dave.

Colman hired Billy, who was fine with the money and whose side he was fighting on made no matter.

The next potential recruit announced by Silva was an Indian, the "Chiricahua Kid," his jaw square, cheekbones high, eyes narrow, and a cold, cold unblinking blue. Ebony hair hung unbraided to his shoulders, his surprisingly tall, narrow frame decked out in a red- and white-man hodgepodge of black sombrero, weathered army jacket, silk bandanna, and knee-high cavalry boots. This "kid" pushing thirty kept a knife high on one hip and a .45 Peacemaker low on the other, and looked every bit as friendly as a rattler, the only difference being this one didn't show his teeth.

Colman told the Indian that he would be expected to kill, sometimes in a general melee on the banks of Sugar Creek, but also might be enlisted for skullduggery.

"What is skullduggery?"

"Back-shooting and throat-slitting."

"White men?"

"Mostly. Maybe a black here or a Mexie there."

"Extra dinero?"

"For that, yes. Would that offend your scruples?"

"What is scruples?"

"Some call it conscience."

The bronze figure thought about that briefly. "Means . . . right and wrong? Yes. This I have."

Not what Colman wanted to hear. "Give me an example of that."

The Apache nodded slowly, then spoke the same way. "Near Fort Grant, woman in small covered wagon sell her ranch. She have boy and baby with her. And money. I shoot her and boy and take money."

Colman blinked. "How the hell's that show me you got scruples?"

The shrug was barely perceptible. "Not rape her. Not kill baby. Later, men say coyotes eat. No right and wrong, coyotes."

Colman hired him on the spot, and then two others, though no other candidates matched the Chiricahua Kid.

That afternoon, Bill Jackson took the chair that earlier had been Clay Colman's, although of course neither man knew of the other's recruiting efforts.

The first candidate, Frank Duffy, was older than Jackson had in mind—well into his forties, but striking nonetheless, six-three easy, and looking even taller because of a ridiculous, somewhat battered top hat. He had broad shoulders and a muscular look, his eyes and hair black, his tanned face narrow and grooved.

Yet he was soft-spoken.

"I have done my share of killing," he said, "but I am no assassin. I have been a soldier fighting Indians and a lawman in Arizona jailing outlaws. So if that disqualifies me, I understand."

"But you ride with the White Caps?"

He frowned, obviously offended. "I do not, sir. I recently took up residence in Las Vegas and have become friendly with Mr. Silva. Despite his . . . sideline, he seems trustworthy."

"Yeah, he does."

"And he is understanding of my frailty."

"What frailty is that?"

He pulled air in, then let it out. "I can get obstreperous when I imbibe. Rest assured I do not drink on the job. However, I may become rowdy after work. I say this openly."

That amused Jackson, who nonetheless said, "This is rough work. You understand that? You'll shoot and be shot at. Give and take no quarter."

Duffy took off the top hat, held it in both hands.

"There was five youngsters, the Scranton brothers, who ran with the Heath rustler gang, who also indulged in holdups. They operated out of Sulphur Valley. In Bisbee they knocked over a mining company store. Half stayed outside, half went in. Alarm went off and indoors shooting commenced. A woman was killed by bullets exiting the front window. My deputy walked up, not knowing the two youngsters outside were part of the gang, and as he headed in to do his duty, they back-shot him. A goodly number of times. My deputy was so dead he didn't have time to know it. What I did in retaliation wasn't strictly legal."

"What was that?"

"Got a lead from a saloon gal that those boys went down to Chihuahua, Mexico, which is where I found them holed up in a bordello. Three I killed in the cantina. Two in bed with wenches. I took no innocent lives, but as I say, my activities were not strictly legal. I lit out. Have not set foot below the border since."

"Is that a true story, old man?"

Duffy went slowly for his gun and Jackson began to rise, but the candidate held out his .44, butt first. Thirteen notches were cut in it.

"The middle five," Duffy said, "are the Scranton brothers."

The story had both convinced and entertained Jackson enough to hire the old boy.

In a vest, collared shirt with loose bow tie, canvas pants with a Colt Lightning .38 worn cross-draw fashion, "Buck" O'Fallon was of medium size but carried himself with a lithe confidence, removing his wide-brimmed hat and planting himself before the seated Jackson.

"Before we start," he began, in a medium-range, flat voice, "you should know I'm not one of Silva's ruffians."

"But you're aware that Silva is not what he pretends to be, to the good citizens of Las Vegas?"

"I am. It's his business. If the 'good citizens' were to hire me to enforce the law, I would make it *my* business. But otherwise . . . no. He's aware of who I am."

"Can't say the same. Who are you?"

A single-shoulder shrug. "Many things. Lawyer for one. Newspaper editor at times. Judge, sheriff, soldier. I've run for office. I have gambled in the various meanings of that word, including the literal, which is what puts me in my current impoverished condition."

"You understand the nature of this work."

"I do."

"You'll kill if need be."

His nod was curt. "If need be. Fired upon I will fire back. Just don't ask ambush of me. That's a line I won't cross."

"Are you the O'Fallon who tracked those train robbers?"

"Tom Horn and I did, yes."

Jackson, like most in the West, knew of legendary tracker Horn.

O'Fallon was saying, "We rode through country few white men had visited. Much gunfire over several weeks was exchanged. I killed one, Tom the other. The brothers split up, so we did, too. Finally I walked into their campsite in Wah Weep Canon, with them sitting round the fire, and just told 'em to stick 'em up. A pair of 'em, that is. They did as told. The other two had gone off another way, and Tom brought them in."

"Four brought back alive."

"And two buried on the trail. That's how it goes in this country. Or anyway, it did. Times do seem to be changing."

Jackson grunted. "Not right now they aren't. You have a job, Mr. O'Fallon."

The man's smile was slight but there. "Call me 'Buck.'"

The two men shook hands.

The final candidate was on the small side, his uncreased black hat riding at an angle, his shirt of the many-buttoned cavalry-style, his trousers duck. On his hip, neither high nor low, rested a Colt .45 Single Action Army revolver—a good choice, Jackson thought.

The slightly cross-eyed young cowboy—and he had the modest stature and bowed legs that made him one—wore a mustache so thick and black it overpowered the rounded-off square of his face. He had a rough, sinewy look, despite his cockeyed look.

"Manning Clements," he said, in a thin, reedy voice that was almost a whine, somewhat at odds with a tough-looking exterior. "Maybe you heard of me."

"Don't believe I have."

"I'm Wes Hardin's cousin."

John Wesley Hardin was, of course, the notorious gunfighter who many considered not just cold-blooded but crazy. Not a relative to be proud of, really.

Jackson filled the prospect in on the job.

Then Jackson asked, "Do you run with the Forty Bandits?"

"I do. I'm one of the White Caps, yessir. And you *need* me for this work."

"Is that right?"

"It is. You see, these others you been talking to, they can handle a gun. But they got no experience with cows. I bossed a trail herd once."

"Mite young for that."

Clements shrugged. "I made mistakes, I grant you."

"Such as?"

He shook his head, laughed at himself. "I hired these boys, Rance and Lou Raine, as drovers. They was miserable and mouthy louts. Caused trouble all the way. Wouldn't work! Just stayed in camp and played cards and ate the grub and slept and such like. I was put out, and finally I said, 'If you'll just go, I'll pay both of you off for the whole shebang, just like you made it to the end of trail. But then git!' They just laughed at me. Then I heard from the other boys that the Raines was talkin' about killin' me. I slept away from camp that night. Hopin' they'd light out."

"Did they?"

He smirked in disgust. "No. And even now I can hear 'em talkin' and laughin'. I lay there and keep thinkin' and thinkin', and I know it's come to a showdown. I went back into camp and shot them sons of bitches."

"In their sleep?"

"No! I woke 'em. It was a . . . a duel, a fair fight. Two against one, but I got them both. I'm fast, Mr. Jackson. And I can shoot. Wes taught me how."

Well, Wes would know.

"And," the infamous gunfighter's cousin said, "it was Wes that got me out of the jam."

Jackson frowned. "With the Raines dead, what jam were you in?"

"Some said it was murder. Among the drovers, you know? So I get word to Wes and he has his friend Bill

Hickok arrest me and stick me in the Abilene hoosegow. Then Wes slips me a key. I was off for Texas before you could spit."

Jackson had his doubts about this one, but the day was dying, so he hired Wes Hardin's cousin on.

At least this hombre was something of a cattleman.

CHAPTER SEVEN

On an unseasonably cold spring afternoon, a small group gathered half a mile north of town on that even stretch of desert known somewhat improbably as Boot Hill. Like a row of massive gravestones, distant buttes provided a somberly beautiful backdrop for the elite group of citizens from Trinidad and the surrounding area who had made their way here by horseback, buggies, and buckboards.

Wearing the same silk mourning dress she'd assumed for her own father's graveside service late last year, Willa Cullen—accompanied by the black foreman who had so recently hired gunfighters to protect her from the woman whose son was being buried—was among those paying respect, though she stood off to one side. In a dark suit, wearing no sidearm but with a rifle handy, Bill Jackson leaned against the buggy and waited.

A disrespectful wind stirred tumbleweed and other brush through the scrubby flat ground, raising a fog of dust that gathered itself at the ankles of mourners. A mesquite tree shivered but otherwise ignored the breeze, resolute in its mission to oversee the wooden crosses and markers and the occasional actual tombstone, for which relatives of a few of the well-off dead had sent away for as far as Denver.

Someone—volunteers from Missionary Baptist, possibly, or perhaps the undertaker and his assistant—appeared to have organized an effort to spruce up the grounds, and to upright any grave indicators knocked over in the brutally hard winter.

As had been the case at her father's service, the entire Citizens Committee—the City Council, they were calling themselves now—were clumped together, with no spouses or offspring accompanying, strung along one side of the grave. This included Mayor Hardy, druggist Davis, hardware man Mathers, mercantile owner Harris, and bank president Burnell. Raymond Parker was there, too. All in their Sunday best.

Noticeably absent was Caleb York.

Not surprising, Willa thought, since Caleb had shot and killed the boy being buried.

A selection of cowhands from the Circle G were on hand, but also noticeably absent were the ranch's rougher customers, some of whom were reportedly veterans of the Earp/Clanton conflict in Tombstone—so-called Cowboys with a capital C. These less threatening cowpunchers were dressed in whatever suit they could manage, hats in hand, awkward yet oddly reverent.

The graveside service had been announced by way of a placard in the undertaker's window. Willa hadn't been sure she should attend. But it was at least a small gesture she could make, a tiny peace offering. Perhaps something human could pass between her and the grieving mother.

Bible in hand, lanky, mutton-chopped Reverend Caldwell stood by the wooden marker, which a Denver tombstone would surely replace, although undertaker Perkins had already provided his best brass-fitted mahogany coffin to designate the importance of the deceased young raper. Beneath the mesquite, Perkins and his adolescent helper waited patiently with two Mexican gravediggers for their turn to take center stage.

"I read to you today from Hebrews two: nine-ten," Caldwell intoned. " 'Yes, by God's grace, Jesus tasted death for everyone. God, for whom and through whom everything was made, chose to bring many children into glory.' "

Along the other side of the grave stood the boy's mother, Victoria Hammond, in a black lace-trimmed satin gown and a mantilla that served as a sort of veil. But the woman's perfectly chiseled features were visible and she showed no signs of tears. Instead her features were so composed as to look frozen, her eyes not on the preacher or the coffin in the hole, but straight ahead.

Next to her were two men in black suits and droopy black bow ties, one on either side, each holding an arm of hers—the woman's sons, someone had whispered to Willa before the proceedings began. One was slender and weepy, and looked to be in his midtwenties and resembled his mother; the other, a few years older, did not. Willa had no way of knowing it, but the older son—burly, firm of jaw, cold of eye—looked like his late father, Andrew Hammond.

The religious words were few. A young woman from the church sang "Amazing Grace." Handfuls of dirt were cast into the grave by each of the three family members. A final prayer and it was over.

Citizens just paying their respects to this new but important player in the area's cattle game (the living mother, not the dead boy) merely nodded and made their way to their horses and conveyances. The city fathers lingered to individually offer their condolences, and bow their heads. Already Victoria Hammond was being paid tribute by Trinidad, which Willa frankly resented, even while feeling mild guilt for such thoughts at the grave site of the woman's youngest son.

The Bar-O's mistress waited until the cemetery had cleared of everyone but the deceased's family and the undertaker with his retinue. The reverend had been the last to go, and could be seen riding alone in a carriage back to town, at an easy pace.

The Hammonds spent no time at William's grave for private thoughts or good-byes. Instead they headed toward a waiting buckboard, watched over by a blond cowboy on horseback—Clay Colman, although he was no one Willa recognized. The cowboy stood out not only because of his good looks, but in being new to the Trinidad environs, at least so far as Willa knew.

She approached the trio in black and Victoria held up a "stop" hand that her sons honored, the younger one almost stumbling to stay in line quickly with his mother.

Willa said, "We have not met, Mrs. Hammond. I'm Willa Cullen." She extended her hand.

The woman accepted it—both wore black lace gloves—and their right hands briefly clasped.

The younger surviving son—whose features were so like his mother's but compressed onto a narrower face, as if the attractiveness had been squeezed out like the juice of a lemon—glared openly at Willa with eyes red from tears.

The older brother seemed bored and didn't look at Willa at all. Nor did he appear to have been crying.

Willa said to the bereaved woman, "You have my sincere condolences," then nodded to each of her attendants. Neither acknowledged her.

"Thank you, Miss Cullen." The voice was almost as low as a man's, yet still quite feminine. "It's kind of you to honor us with your presence. Were you acquainted with my brother? Had you met?"

Willa shook her head, offered up a sad smile. "No. He was pointed out to me in town, on the street. He was a handsome lad. I'm very sorry."

No grief whatsoever showed on the beautiful face. "The circumstances were . . . unfortunate."

Willa nodded. "It adds a bitterness to the passing. I lost my father last year, to violence. He lies here in this same ground."

"A rather desolate resting place, don't you think?"

Wind rustled the mesquite's leaves. Tumbleweed tumbled.

"It is that," Willa granted. She gestured toward the cliffs. "But there's beauty on the horizon."

The Hammond woman nodded, just a little. "Poetically put. And I'm glad to finally meet you, Miss Cullen, since we *do* have business."

"Yes. But, of course, this is not the time or place . . ."

"Fifty cents an acre."

". . . Pardon?"

The big dark eyes fixed upon her. Stared, really.

"For your land," the woman said, "and the stock on it. You may keep the house and its outbuildings, barn, corrals, and such." She tossed a black-gloved hand. "Call it half an acre."

Willa backed up a step, almost as if she'd been slapped. "Mrs. Hammond, please don't make me respond in these circumstances."

"Why not?"

The younger son was smiling. The older one seemed not to be listening.

Willa frowned at the woman. "You know very well that your offer is outrageously low."

The owner of the Circle G held up a gloved palm. "Your stock are skin and bones and their numbers greatly reduced. Without access to clean water, they will certainly die. Bloated carcasses will again pepper your range, even without another season of snow."

Spine stiffening, chin rising, Willa said, "I have no desire to sell, Mrs. Hammond. We Cullens have been on the Bar-O since—"

"Your father stole the land from the Indians?"

Willa felt her cheeks reddening. "He did no such thing. He bought it from the Mexican government."

"Ah. With money he made killing the buffalo and starving the savages out. In any case, they needed clearing out. Such men built this country, Miss Cullen. You should be proud. . . . It's a good offer."

"It's an insulting offer."

Victoria Hammond touched her bosom with splayed fingers. "Please. I'd rather not squabble with my boy lying so freshly dead in his grave."

Tamping down her irritation, Willa said, "You are buying up the small ranches. Soon you'll have a spread almost as large as the Bar-O. We need not be adversaries. You will require access to the Purgatory, where it runs through my land. There's no reason for us not to be good neighbors."

Now the dark eyes were lidded. "Without access to Sugar Creek, you will soon be bankrupt. It's not my fault that you are a bad businesswoman."

This time Willa didn't rise to the bait.

"I apologize for getting into this at such a delicate time," she said. "I understand you're distressed."

But Willa knew this woman wasn't distressed in the least.

Willa turned away, looking back over her shoulder to say, "We'll meet later, under more appropriate circumstances."

As Willa neared the road at the cemetery's edge, the mourning mother called out, "I note that your friend Caleb York did not honor us with his presence, despite having made this gathering today possible! At least you, my dear, have a sense of propriety."

Willa wheeled to speak, but could find no words, and then Bill Jackson was helping her up into the carriage and they were heading back to the Bar-O with the foreman on the whip. But Willa was unnerved by the encounter, and especially by what she'd seen when she'd looked back to almost make one last remark to the woman.

Victoria Hammond had been smiling, even as the Mexicans with shovels were heading toward her son's grave.

In the library of the Circle G ranch house, at the opposite end of the room from Victoria Hammond's desk, mutton-chopped Andrew Hammond seemed to glower down in judgment from the imposing oil painting on the wall. Below was a love seat in the Spanish style, warm dark wood with red velvet and gold-embroidered upholstery, in which sat the late William Hammond's mother. In matching armchairs opposite, against respective walls, were her sons.

They were dressed in the same somber black as at the

cemetery. Coffee had been served by the help and three untouched cups were growing cold on a low-slung table. The older son, Hugh, was looking straight ahead, at nothing. The younger son, Pierce, her middle boy, was gazing at his mother, his expression twitchy, expectant. Her arms were extended along the upper back of the settee.

Finally she spoke.

"Hugh," she said, turning her eyes on her older son.

He looked at her. His expression seemed less than loving, but stopped short of insolence.

"You were raised on two ranches," she said.

He said nothing. This of course was not news to him.

"Wyoming as a boy," she continued, "Colorado as a young man. You did well enough, but your father and I sensed other things for you. So we sent you east for schooling, and you excelled. You returned and soon evidenced a real talent for business. And you have done well as the president of the Trinidad bank."

That was the Trinidad, Colorado, bank.

"I am proud," she went on. "But due to no fault on your part, the bank is failing. As was the case with so many businesses, the winter did us in."

He said nothing. This younger version of the man looming in the oil painting seemed bored by such a pointless recitation of the obvious.

"It is my intention," she said, "to install you here at my right hand. My bookkeeper, Byers, has done well enough, in the interim . . . but he is not family. He is not blood. And he does not possess your acumen, Hugh."

Her older son again said nothing.

She continued to level her gaze at him. "We have acquired almost all of the smaller ranches. And as you saw, this afternoon, we are moving forward with our expansion efforts."

And now the older boy spoke: "That young woman—who owns the Bar-O?"

"Willa Cullen. Yes?"

"Don't underestimate her."

Victoria laughed lightly. "She's just a child. Snip of a thing."

Her older son shook his head. Slowly. He had his father's gray eyes. "No. She's strong. Men underestimate you, Mother, because you're a beautiful woman. Don't make the same mistake about the Cullen girl."

Victoria rose and began to pace slowly in front of the towering portrait. "I have already taken steps to deal with her and her ragtag troops. You'll meet my foreman, Clay Colman, soon. He has experience in such things."

"You mean he's a rustler and a gunfighter."

She stopped in front of her older boy. "Yes. He'll be vital in our efforts to restock. To rebuild. There's much to do. This spread, and all of the little ones we've swallowed up, were hit almost as hard by the Die-Up as were we, north of here. The answer lies to the south."

Behind her, the younger son, Pierce, said, "Mexico?"

She turned to him, cast a fond smile on the son she loved most, but knew was the least. "Mexico. You will ride with Mr. Colman. You will be his right hand."

Pierce's face tightened, almost crinkled, as if tears were coming; but that wasn't the case—he just often seemed to look as if about to cry. "He should be *my* right hand, Mother! *I'll* be the Hammond on these drives!"

She glided to him, touched his cheek with a black lace–gloved hand. "Yes, dear one, but he is older and more experienced, and you have much to learn. Your time will come. It will come."

"You always say that, Mother, but . . ."

"It. Will. Come."

Left unsaid was something all three of them knew, although Pierce did not like to admit it to himself: Though he, too, had been raised on their ranches, and he could follow orders, he had no real leadership skills. Nor had there been any thought of sending *him* east to college. Or west, for that matter.

The youngest brother, William, had been a natural when it came to ranching—he could cowboy with the best of them. And he was liked, and got listened to. But he had inherited his father's drinking ways and certain other less than noble habits—like the randy inclinations that had gotten him killed—and her ambitions for William, her hopes, her dreams, were buried with him now.

Victoria began to slowly pace again, gesturing gently as she spoke. "The day will come, my sons, when you, Hugh, will be at the helm of businesses and banks and more, as we grow and prosper. And you, Pierce, will one day take over this ranch. Together you boys will become everything your father once was. . . ."

Everything, that is (she desperately hoped), *except those dark qualities her dead youngest son had inherited.*

"I won't disappoint you, Mother," Pierce said, on the edge of the beautiful, uncomfortable chair.

"I know you won't, dear," she said offhandedly.

Victoria turned to face her oldest son, who looked so much like his father had on their first meeting so many years ago. She approached him.

"Now," she said, "as to the matter of the man who murdered your brother. Caleb York."

Hugh's eyebrows went up, slightly. "Murdered?"

She frowned. "Could it be called anything else?"

He shrugged. "A lawman performing his duty?"

"How can you say that!"

"My understanding, Mother, is that our rash brother raped and thrashed some poor Mexican girl, and was hiding behind another *muchacha* when this sheriff came round to arrest him."

"Yes. And?"

He frowned. "There *is* no 'and' . . . York stopped William, who it very much sounds like needed stopping."

Her nostrils flared. "Did you not *hear* me? I agreed it was just some Mexican girl!"

"Yes, and a *puta* at that. You know—like your *mother* once was . . . our dear departed grandmother?"

She shook a forefinger at him, as so many before her had done with a child who sassed. "You need to watch what you say to me, Hugh Hammond!"

His manner was infuriatingly casual. "I don't much care whether our brother had his way with some tramp and beat her half to death, either. But, drunk, he was stupid. He was careless. And it's a streak that's in you, too, Mother dear." His eyes landed hard on his sibling across the way. "And *you,* brother."

Pierce's mouth came open, but no words found their way out.

"That 'streak' you talk about," Victoria said, leaning toward her seated older son, "is in the Hammond blood! It's what made your father a force to be reckoned with in the cattle trade!"

Hugh looked up at her, his expression blasé. "No. That was another kind of streak—call it a talent for larceny. A gift for doing whatever ruthless damn thing it takes to get ahead. A knack for putting knives in the backs of business associates and friends. *That* was the streak that made him a cattle baron, Mother. It's that other streak of his that brought Papa down—his reckless-ness. His arrogant thinking that he could do anything he liked, take whatever he wanted, and get away with it . . . while *not* getting himself killed. But of course someone managed it, nonetheless." His eyes rose to the portrait dominating them all. "We never knew *who* was responsi-ble, did we?"

Her chin lifted. "No. Whoever murdered your father was never identified."

Hugh flipped a hand. "Well, of course, I was away at school when it happened. But I heard rumors. I heard stories."

"Did you."

He nodded. "I did. Whoever it was, though, I don't blame them. Papa used to beat Pierce, you know. And he beat his women, too, when he tired of them. So the world suffered no great loss when Andrew Hammond . . . shuf-fled off this mortal coil, as John Wilkes Booth once said."

"Edwin," Pierce corrected quietly.

Victoria's words came soft but screamed somehow. "William was just a boy."

"Ah," Hugh said, "but what a boy. He had Papa's streak, all right. And you know which one."

She spoke through her teeth. "You would let Caleb York get away with . . . with killing your own *brother*? However justified the law of little men might find it?"

Nodding several times, he said, "Yes, Mother. I would. I definitely would."

Wearing a small but distinct sneer, she said, "Well, then, leave it to me. You don't need to soil yourself with vengeance. I will handle things myself."

Hugh gave up half a smirk. "You mean, you will, with the help of your latest . . . ramrod? I'm sure you will,

Mother. As for me, I have other things to do. Other than more cattle rustling and helping you build another 'empire.' "

Her chin went back and her eyes came down. "Why did you even bother to come home then?"

He rose. "Is that what this is? Home? First time I've seen it, yet it's so, so familiar. Mother, I came home to say good-bye to my sad little got-himself-killed baby brother. I loved the rascal. He didn't deserve my affection, but, as you say, it's blood. And Pierce . . . I've always had a soft spot for him, too. He's gentle underneath, he just doesn't know it."

"Stop this." She bit off the words. "I'll hear no more of it."

"Oh, I'm done. Really done. But I came home to say good-bye to you, too, Mother . . . and to him." He nodded up at the painting. "Of course, I have to see his damn face in the mirror every time I shave. It's enough to make a man grow a full-face beard."

"You'll come back. Crawling."

"On my hands and knees, you think? No, I'm quite capable of staying upright. You see, one of the reasons our bank is failing is that I've helped myself, some. Don't bother looking for what I took, because it's safely deposited in banks back East. That's where you sent me for my learning, Mother. But, really, I learned quite a lot from you and Papa. . . . I'll be taking a horse into town and checking into the hotel. I'll leave it in the livery stable. You didn't raise me to be a thief, after all."

He went out, smiling, a lightness in his step.

Pierce was at her side. "Mother, I will never, would *never* do that. Never walk out on you. Never, *ever* let you down."

"I know you won't, darling."

Of course, the boy had never done anything in his life *but* let her down. Still, why hurt his feelings? She was too good a mother for that.

"I'm all for killing Caleb York, Mother. All for it!"

At least, she thought, *his heart's in the right place.*

CHAPTER EIGHT

Caleb York sat at his desk in his office working with a fountain pen on the ledger that recorded taxes collected and rewards paid (two separate sections of the big orange-black–spined book). He would fill the pen from time to time from an inkwell. Not yet proficient at it, he occasionally got ink on his hand, keeping a handkerchief handy, and now and then a black blob made the record book look like the work of a small child.

Keeping up with change wasn't easy.

He was putting the ledger away in his middle desk drawer when Tulley rushed in, looking to burst.

"Sheriff!" the skinny, bandy-legged deputy said, louder than need be since the old boy was standing right in front of the desk now. "Trouble be stirrin' out t' Sugar Crick."

Tulley, who had long since abandoned his desert-rat rags at the sheriff's direction, was resplendent in navy flannel shirt, red suspenders, gray woolen pants, and work boots.

"What were you doing out that way, Tulley?"

"I *weren't* out there! No sir! But it's the God's honest truth."

York folded his hands, his right one sharing ink with his left. "How do you come by this?"

The deputy looked left and looked right, making sure no one in the empty office and the nearby vacant jail cell might overhear. He closed one eye and opened the other, wide. "I were bellied up to the bar, partakin' of nothin' stronger than a sarsaparilly, I will have ye know—ain't fell off the wagon yet, Caleb York."

"I know, Tulley. Admirable."

This time the deputy looked right, and looked left, checking for eavesdroppers again. Then he cackled. "I guess I needn't tell ye I got ears like a fox! And I keeps 'em to the ground."

Vivid as those words were, they failed to conjure any image in York's mind.

"To the unschooled eye," Tulley was saying, "all I be doin' was jest chewin' the fat with ol' Hub, who is gettin' a mite portly, I come to notice. Best lay off the gravy and taters, sez I."

The deputy referred to Hub Wainright, the burly, sparsely mustached bouncer/bartender at the saloon.

"The point, Tulley."

He pointed a gnarled finger at the outside. "Jest down the bar, some cowboys from this spread and that 'un was jawin' over beer. Seems the widower Hammond hired herself some guns to keep them Bar-O cowpunchers from waterin' their beeves over to Sugar Crick."

"You mean her cowmen are armed." York shrugged. "That doesn't surprise me."

Tulley shook his head and wisps of white danced. "No, no—these ain't your ever'day cowhands, jes' packin' some lead. These is *kill*-fighters. Murder for money boys. Is what these fellers claimed, anyways. Over suds it be, but still."

York opened the bottom right-hand drawer of his desk and got out his bullet-studded gun belt and Colt Single Action .44.

"Best I ride out and have a look," York said. "The grapevine's probably just picked up on those Arizona boys who signed on. Rough customers, but not hired guns."

Tulley leaned in. "What *I* heered, Caleb York, it was *jest* that—gunhands hired for killin'! And that ain't the *worst* of it."

York was strapping on the gun belt. "What is, then?"

Tulley pointed to the outside again. "Miz Cullen, she follered suit. She's got herseff some gunfighters that was hired on by that colored foreman of hern. If scuttlebutt's to be believed, them gun-toters was rounded up, up Las Vegas way. Still a mean town, that. Parts of it, anyways."

York was heading toward the door. "You did good, Deputy. Hold down the fort."

Tulley's smile had a surprising number of teeth left in it. "Don't I always? We ain't been raided yet."

Always a first time, York thought grimly. *Especially if a range war is brewing . . .*

The day was warm enough that York decided to leave his black frock coat behind, vest too, and left the office tugging his hat on and with his sheriff's badge pinned to his gray shirt with the pearl buttons. The badge was something he wanted seen by the woman he was calling on, and by anybody working for her. Same went for his Colt revolver.

York rode the twenty minutes or so out to the Circle G, where he again found the corral empty and the handful of frame buildings showing no sign of life. The cowhands were *somewhere*—still out on the range dealing with stinking dead cattle and skinny live ones, maybe.

Or possibly beyond that stand of firs in back of the ranch house, on the banks of Sugar Creek, armed and ready. . . .

As York tied the dappled gray gelding up at the hitching rail, the Hammond woman's portly bookkeeper—his gray suit about the same color as his handlebar mustache—came down the two steps from the low-riding porch.

"Mr. Byers," York said.

"Sheriff," Byers said pleasantly, though his eyes crinkled suspiciously. "The mistress is out on the patio. If you'll wait here, I'll announce you."

Seemed to be no question that he'd be received.

Soon York—hat in hand, .44 on his hip—was again being shown through the house, with its framed western landscapes, dark Spanish furnishings, and colorful Mexican carpets. French doors in the living room opened onto a flagstone courtyard with a small gurgling fountain at its center, potted plants hugging the walls on the periphery, and a eucalyptus tree providing shade in one corner.

Beneath that tree, in an oak and saddle-leather armchair with a footstool she wasn't using, sat Victoria Hammond, reading a book, its cover the same brown as the chair, its title *The Portrait of a Lady*.

Byers deposited York there, then nodded and was gone.

As York approached, his hostess smiled, dog-eared the corner of the page she was on, and closed the volume. "Are you familiar with Henry James, Sheriff York?"

Victoria Hammond wore a white high-collar, button-down blouse and long black skirt—half of her, at least, was still in mourning.

"Never met the man," York said.

"I refer to the author." She put the book down on a small table at her right hand. "Perhaps you're not a reader."

She gestured to the footstool for him to sit, and he did, pulling it around to one side, though of course that still put her over him. The big dark eyes were trained down on him, as if the teacher were hoping against hope to get a good response from a slow student.

"Not a bookworm, no," York admitted. "And I'm more an H. Rider Haggard man myself. Robert Louis Stevenson comes up with some good tales. You familiar with *Dr. Jekyll and Mr. Hyde?*"

She seemed amused. "I can't say that I am."

"Well, it's a pretty good yarn. Don't read it 'fore bedtime, though."

Her eyebrows rose a bit. "Could I offer you something to drink?"

"Got a mite dry riding out here. Some water, maybe?"

"I'm partial to lemonade. Would you like a glass?"

His last glass of that stuff had been at Willa's.

"Kind of you," he said.

A pretty young Mexican señorita in red-trimmed white appeared magically and Victoria said, "*Dos limonada,*" and the serving girl nodded and disappeared.

Victoria Hammond's luminous, almost ebony eyes were still appraising him, her arms folded beneath the generous shelf of her breasts. "What brings you by the Circle G this afternoon, Sheriff?"

He sat there awkwardly, knees in the air, hat between his legs. "Well, first, my apologies for not attending your son's services. I thought under the circumstances, it . . . uh, wouldn't be appropriate."

She waved that off. "Nor are apologies necessary, Caleb. Instinctively, you knew that paying respects under, as you say, such circumstances might have provided more pain than succor. I appreciate your sensitivity."

He risked only a corner of a smile. "That's not something I'm often accused of, Mrs. Hammond."

Her smile took no such precaution. "Please. I've taken the liberty of calling you by *your* Christian name. Mine is Victoria."

The servant girl brought two clear glass cups with handles in which ice chips floated in pale yellow liquid. He thanked the girl, which the hostess did not, and sipped. Nicely tart. Like Willa's.

Victoria's chin lifted slightly. "So, Caleb—is this a social call? Are we to be friends now? I'm sure there are those who would find that unlikely. Or perhaps . . . as you say, not appropriate."

On the footstool, he felt like a supplicant child. "I'm afraid it's official, uh, Victoria. Or on the fringes of such, anyway."

"How so?"

He jumped right in. "My deputy overheard some cowboys—not from the Circle G—saying both you and Willa Cullen have hired on men with guns."

She sipped the cool liquid. Smiled. The smile was tart, too. "Don't *most* men in this part of the world have guns? With so many dangerous . . . *creatures* afoot, even a female of the species might be well served to know her way around a firearm. Which, frankly, I do."

"I'm not surprised. Nor do I think it unwise. But what I'm talking about, Victoria, are hired guns. Killers."

She nodded toward the firearm at his side, which as he perched on the stool was only staying in its holster because the weapon was strapped in.

"*You* wear a gun, Caleb," she said. "You have killed. In fact, you're famous for it."

"I'm not proud of the fact." He shook his head. "But I've never been one of these shootists for hire."

Both dark eyebrows went up. "Why, was it a *hobby* for you?"

He chuckled, knowing he was being mocked, if gently. "No, ma'am. I was paid by Wells Fargo. Now I'm paid by taxpayers like yourself. And the township of Trinidad."

"Ah. Then, you *are* a hired gun."

"But not a gun who hires out to just anyone."

"I don't care to think of myself as just anyone, Caleb." She sat forward, casting her dark gaze down on him as if lining up a shot. "But you are definitely . . . shall we say . . . on target? When you point out that I am a taxpayer, that is. And, of course, those taxes pay you to uphold the law. Am I not right?"

"That's right."

She gestured gracefully with an open hand. "And I *have* hired some men known for their skill and their daring with pistols and rifles. Many were once soldiers. As, I believe, *you* were, once upon a time."

"I was, Victoria. But it was no fairy tale."

Her tone was casual, though her expression was not. "You are, I believe, aware of the water rights disagreement between Miss Cullen and myself."

"I am."

"Miss Cullen feels, I understand, that certain agreements between neighboring ranchers, made long ago and never formalized, should be honored by the new owner of the Circle G, who happens to be me. Clean, clear water is at this moment a scarcity in these parts. At a premium, you might say. Sugar Creek runs through my land. It's *near* her property, yes . . . but it cuts through mine alone."

He raised palms of surrender. "This sounds like something you two should sit down and work out. Or law book men who represent you. It doesn't have to come to guns."

Her smile looked sad, or tried to. "Ah, but Caleb—you said it yourself. She has hired her own gunmen. Her own 'soldiers.' That is her prerogative, of course. Perhaps she wants such men merely to guard her land—to keep her scrawny, barely breathing livestock from being 'rustled,' as they say. Or perhaps she fears the Apaches will rise up again and her home must be protected."

"You and I both know neither is likely."

The teacher lifted a scolding forefinger. "That, Caleb, is my point. The Cullen girl has assembled this little army solely to *invade* the Circle G." She shrugged rather grandly. "So I have every right to assemble an army of my own. I have a right, a *duty*, to defend myself and my property. Stand your ground is a privilege, even a golden rule here in the Southwest. You know it, and I know it."

What could he say to that?

He had another sip of the tart drink and stood. Deposited the glass on the little table. "Are you suggesting I stay out of this? Let the 'armies' fight it out?"

Now she was looking up at him. "Have you another suggestion?"

"I can't say I do. I can only say I wish you two females would find some other way to work this thing out besides lettin' bullets fly."

He nodded to her and started out.

Then in a rustle of feminine fabric she was at his side and holding on to his arm. Under her long dress she may have been wearing boots that put her at his eye level like this, but there was no denying that, even so, for a female she was a tall drink of water.

Or maybe lemonade.

She said, "I have to disagree with you, Caleb. Because you're clearly shirking your duty."

Their eyes locked.

"My duty," he said, "is to try and shut this powder-burning contest down before all of you wind up losers."

Victoria shook her head gently, her eyes staying steady. She was near to him. "No. You were right first time."

"Right how?"

"That I'm a taxpayer. Your side in this is with me."

He frowned. "Willa Cullen is a taxpayer, too."

"I don't deny that. I'm sure she's quite scrupulous in that regard. But if she crosses over into my property, and waters her cattle in my stream, without my say-so . . . without negotiating water rights, which *I* hold . . . your responsibility is to protect me and *mine*."

The frown went deeper. "You expect me to back you up over Willa?"

"As long as you wear that badge I do, yes." She came ever closer to him, face-to-face. She still smelled like lilacs, damn her. Her breasts were pressed against his chest and her nostrils flared and so did her eyes, like a horse rearing and begging to be broke.

"I would not insult you," she said, "by offering you money. But I *would* be grateful. And I would find some way . . . to show it."

Her face came up and her mouth found his. They were soft and supple, those full, sensual lips, and slowly moved with his, speaking to him silently, expressing an unmistakable yearning. His first reaction was surprise, and yet he didn't draw away from her. He let her do what she wanted to, and then his arms went around her and held her even closer. When she drew away, just barely, he grabbed her and held her to him and kissed her again, harder. Almost savagely.

Then he pushed her away. "You don't have to bribe me, woman. And I know just what I should do. What my responsibility is."

Her head went back, her eyes looked down; even standing, she was somehow above him. "I'm within my rights, Caleb. I'm acting within the law."

"I know."

His heart was beating fast and he was offended and ex-hilarated, angry and delighted, and—as he left and moved through the house, past the servant girl—he was glad he hadn't put his hat on, holding it before him just below the belt.

Outside, he leaned against his horse and considered what needed doing, and how. Byers came out after a while.

"Sheriff," he said, approaching him. "Are you all right?"

York turned to the bookkeeper. "How far to where the Circle G men are camped?"

"Just through the stand of firs," he said, gesturing that way. "About half a mile."

"How far coming around along the creek, from the north?"

Byers shrugged. "Few miles."

"And from the south?"

"Same."

"Any idea how long it might take? I'm not that famil-iar with the lay of this land."

The bookkeeper shook his head. "I'm no horseman. Be easier to walk it."

"I'm going to leave my horse here." York patted the animal and withdrew his Winchester 1873 from its saddle scabbard. "That acceptable, Mr. Byers?"

"I'm sure the mistress won't mind. She's a law-biding woman."

That didn't rate a response.

He walked around the hacienda-style ranch house and strode across the shallow backyard, the Winchester by its stock in his left hand, nose angled down. Then he was in the stand of firs, though it was more than just a stand really, more a patch of forest on gradually sloping ground.

Moving through, he had to step around one tall pine after another, as no path was there to help him. The process was serpentine, the journey a weaving one, but he felt a calm settle over him, after living so long in the midst of so much desert; it was soothing somehow to have his boots cracking dry brown needles and crunching fallen leaves, though the occasional outgrown root made the going bumpy.

Swords of sunlight cut through cool blue shadows, while birds called and pecked as smaller animals scurried and stopped and scurried some more. With the ground still damp from the winter, he could smell pine resin and leaves and loam and minty grass, as the rush of the stream up ahead made itself known and then became more and more dominant.

Then came the sound of men, and ruined it.

He paused where the pines gave way to a steeper grassy incline that fell a few feet to more green before the dramatic white of the sandy bank of Sugar Creek. Along the tree line, horses were tied up, their whinnies and neighing punctuating the flow of water. That bleached beach of perhaps five feet of width was despoiled by half a dozen cowboys milling, smoking, many with the heel of their hands on the butts of low-slung guns.

Closer to York, on the grass, were two campsites, separated by perhaps twelve feet, where wood was piled, awaiting a nighttime fire, not needed for many hours yet, the sun high and glinting off the nearby sand and shimmering on the gently rolling stream. Across the water was nothing but another ribbon of white with a rocky rise to scrubby trees. No one was over there, at the moment, not that could be seen anyway.

On this side, at least a dozen men were either sitting around the pair of cold campfires or just on their haunches on the grassy slope to the left and right of where York emerged. He'd seen plenty of them before, knew many by name. The Circle G, ever since the days when it was in the late Sheriff Harry Gauge's hands, had been home to a rough damn bunch of cowhands—rabble and rustlers to a man.

Added in were the Arizona Cowboys who had been lately hired on—"cowboys" with a capital C, which might also have stood for Clanton. These survivors of the Tombstone ruckus had rustled and robbed and even now wore their trademark rattlesnake hatband—either a silver version some jeweler pounded out or an actual rattlesnake skin.

This bunch of dead-eyed, sneering back-shooters, added to the Gauge residue, constituted about the scruffiest collection of supposed ranch hands York had ever seen.

But then that was the West, wasn't it? The Earps had been gamblers as well as guardians of the law, pimps and protectors of civilization, horse thieves and posse men after stagecoach robbers. Many considered Caleb York a killer as bad as any of the human flotsam and jetsam scattered about this white beach like the aftermath of a drunken bacchanal.

No, *worse*—York had killed more men in his time than any three of these lowlifes combined. Any four.

So who am I to talk? he thought.

With his Winchester gripped in his left hand, York stepped out from the trees and eased down the grassy slope, a couple dozen or so eyes fixing on him with the usual love bad men reserved for men wearing badges.

He nodded to a few, and they would pause but nod back, eyes narrow with suspicion, contempt, or both. A figure approached York, someone he did not recognize at first; then it came to him—Clay Colman, who'd been suspected in a robbery that York investigated for Wells Fargo.

York had never quite got the goods on Colman, but had gunned down the other two suspects—a close shave, as they'd both pulled on him at the same time.

Colman was a good-looking, strapping son of a bitch, blond, blue-eyed, with sharp features and a black hat sporting, yes, a rattlesnake hatband. Genuine rattlesnake, at that.

"Mr. Colman," York said. With a nod and a tight smile.

"Sheriff," Colman said. With a nod and a tight smile.

Neither man even thought about shaking hands.

"I understand," York said, "you're the Circle G ramrod now."

His smile was barely there. "I am. Miz Hammond is a hell of a boss, for a woman."

York gave him a similar smile back. "From what I see, she'd make a hell of a boss for a man . . . though I don't imagine anybody'd mistake her for one."

"No. No indeed." Colman pushed his hat back on his head, his hands going to his hips. "How can I help you, Sheriff?"

"Well, I see a few familiar faces among your crew. Some Arizona boys, from back in those days."

"True enough."

"And a couple that don't strike me as your average cowpoke. Isn't that Billy Bassett over there?"

York pointed off to the left to a skinny mustached character, a Remington revolver low on his hip.

"Yep," Colman said.

Then the sheriff pointed off to the right, indicating a guy of medium height in a dark suit, training his close-set eyes across the glimmering stream. "That's Dave Carson, right? He's worked both sides of the law. But then many have."

"Yep," Colman said.

"And up ahead of us, that one's pretty unmistakable—the Chiricahua Kid himself." York nodded toward the muscular Indian in the army jacket and black sombrero, who—like the other two he'd pointed out—was staring across the strip of water like a hawk. A hungry one.

"Yep," Colman said. "We don't hold no grudge against the red man."

"That particular one didn't leave many alive *to* hold a grudge."

Colman nodded. "Probably not any, y'get down to it."

"Those three gents stand out, and not just 'cause you have 'em positioned all along this stretch of sand."

"Stand out how, Sheriff?"

"They kill for money."

"Like soldiers."

York nodded a few times. "You could say that. But I'm here in hopes of keepin' a war from breakin' out. What's your intention, should the Bar-O boys herd their stock to this stream?"

Colman flipped a hand toward Sugar Creek. "My notion, since you ask, is to start shootin' into the air. That'll rile the beeves, and they'll start stampedin'. Who can say which way they'll go? But if they head back from whence they come, well, that's fine. Some'll likely scatter off down the shore, in one direction or t'other, and them Bar-O cowboys can earn their pay roundin' 'em up."

York squinted at the ramrod. "What if some of them cows head *this* way? If you shoot those strays on the swim, you'll foul your own water source. What if that stampede heads for these pines, with your boss lady's ranch house in back of there? You want those steers in her lap?"

Colman grunted a laugh. "You ain't a cattleman, are you, York? Ain't gonna go that way. The water'd slow 'em down, and then we got a whole mess of cowboys on hand to round 'em up. Any steer makes it into the pines will be slowed down by 'em, and we'll pick them up, too."

"To rustle them, you mean. And use a branding iron to change G to O?"

Colman grinned. "Now we're gettin' a mite ahead of ourselves, Sheriff."

"*Clay!*"

It was Bassett. He was pointing across the way. "*Here they come!*"

Through those scrubby trees emerged men on horseback. They were not riding hard—the landscape didn't lend itself to that. But they were soon lined up all along the grassy stretch above the white bank opposite, reining their horse back with one hand, a handgun in the other.

In the middle, in the lead, was Bill Jackson. Among many other familiar faces from the Bar-O bunkhouse were three newcomers—York knew at once these were the gunfighters Willa had enlisted. The three killers on horseback were spaced out much as Colman's were . . .

Frank Duffy, a sometime lawman, broad of shoulder, hard of eye, oldest man here and tallest in a battered top hat that emphasized that height.

"Buck" O'Fallon, not big, not small, an erudite fellow who had also once worn a badge, his hat wide brimmed, his bow tie loose and floppy.

And—most disturbingly—Manning Clements, the cock-eyed cousin of that deadly loco gunman John Wesley Hardin, who Manning had devoted much of his misguided life to emulating.

York brushed Colman aside and walked down through the Circle G boys, all of whom stood with hands hovering over holstered handguns, and walked right up to the water's edge. The beautiful flowing stream sparkled with sunlight, oblivious to the tension it was engendering.

As their horses danced in place, Jackson was in the midst of his men, with Clements beside him. York assumed that was because Jackson likely realized how dangerous Hardin's cousin was and wanted to keep an eye on him.

"Bill," York called out, and it echoed across the water, "you know who I am—and for anyone who doesn't, I'm Caleb York, sheriff of San Miguel County! You are on Circle G land. Return to the Bar-O! I intend to solve this conflict peaceably!"

Jackson yelled back, *"We are not here to fight! Not today. We only want to send a message."*

"What message?"

"That if a shooting war need be, we are armed and ready. All we ask is to water our stock before they die of thirst."

"Guns won't settle this."

"*Whose side are you on, Caleb York?*"

"The law. The county. And right now you're trespassing, and you need to ride off and let this matter take its lawful course."

"*What if that bunch starts shooting first?*"

"Whoever does that, on whichever side, deals with me! I am right now asking both groups to retreat. To disperse. Until this can be resolved the right way."

In days to come—even in years to pass—conflicting accounts and arguments on either side would wage a war of words over what happened next. But at that moment words weren't the ammunition.

Manning Clements's right arm stretched out with his Colt .45 in his fist and the crack echoed across the stream.

Caleb York drew his .44 and returned fire.

When the bullet entered Manning's forehead, the impact briefly uncrossed the man's eyes and sent him tumbling off the horse, dead before he hit the grassy, sandy ground.

CHAPTER NINE

A terrible two seconds passed in which general gunfire might have broken out and carnage would have stained scarlet the white banks on either side of Sugar Creek.

Perhaps it was the rearing of the horses under the Bar-O boys that prevented the third second from being filled with blood and gunsmoke. Maybe it was Willa's crew already having their guns in hand that gave the Circle G crowd momentary pause, or possibly the frantic, unsettling whinnies and neighs of the horses behind them, tied to pines.

Finally it was Caleb York himself moving to the very edge of the water—holding a palm out behind him to the men whose hands hovered over their sidearms—as he shouted, "Collect your men and go, Jackson! Or there'll be nothing but dead men left to do it."

Jackson, still settling his horse, said nothing, but to his credit he too was signaling his men with an upraised palm to hold back.

Then the Bar-O foreman shouted, "*You'll have to answer for this, Sheriff!*"

York's voice echoed across the stream, which ran along on its almost languid way, untouched by human conflict. "Tell your mistress I will call on her yet today! If there's to be killing, let it wait!"

The tension in the air was palpable—the Bar-O riders with their guns trained, the Circle G men on their feet with hands over holstered weapons.

The horse under him steady now, Jackson climbed down and, with the help of another cowhand, draped the body of Manning Clements over the dead man's saddle. Jackson spoke to his helper, who nodded, and then was heading back through the scrubby trees leading the corpse's horse.

"*This don't end it!*" Jackson called, ready to ride again.

And with a sweeping hand motion, the foreman led the cowpunchers and the two remaining gunhands away, with only scowls thrown back at their opponents and, thankfully, not bullets.

The rough bunch on the Circle G shore laughed and boasted and milled, and several came over to slap the sheriff on the back. York—relieved though he was to have limited this encounter to one fatality—was in no mood for congratulation.

Then Colman was at his side, for once wearing neither smirk nor sneer, but in no celebratory mood, either. "This ain't over."

"Not by a long shot," York agreed.

Now half a grin formed. "Speakin' of which, Sheriff, that was a *hell* of a shot. Just don't tell me you were aimin' for the horse."

"No."

Colman looked narrow-eyed at York. "At this distance, you went for a head shot with a six-gun?"

York was staring across the stream, where the only sign of the riders now were some puffs of dust and a splotch of red on the grassy, sandy incline.

He said, "I pretty much always go for a head shot."

"Interestin' choice," Colman said. "Kinda risky, though. Chest gives you a bigger target. That's always my inclination."

"Head-shot men don't return fire. But the next time that Bar-O bunch comes around, you can bet *they* will." York shifted his gaze to the ramrod. "I don't suppose I can convince you to break this party up. Maybe leave a couple of men at your campfires to keep an eye out."

"If I do anything," Colman said, "it'll be t'bring the rest of the G's punchers in from the range, and spread this armed camp out farther to the north and south."

"Fuel to the fire."

"Maybe so, but we didn't light it." Colman's chin came up. "You're right about this much, York—they'll be back and they will be shooting."

"Maybe not. I do intend to talk to Willa Cullen, yet today. Maybe this loss of a life will get her to see reason." York allowed himself a sigh. "I would appreciate it if you'd do the same with Mrs. Hammond."

The ramrod shook his head. "Can't do that, Sheriff."

"Why in hell not?"

The ramrod shrugged. "Against my best interests. I wasn't just hired to do a foreman's job, you know. I could lie to you and say otherwise, but what's the point?"

"None. We both know Victoria Hammond took you on as much for your gunfighter skills as your cattle know-how."

Colman turned toward the pines that separated them from the ranch house. His hands were on his hips. "Now that we know they're coming, I'll only post lookouts on the shore. Rest of us will be in the trees. With our rifles. It will be a damn slaughter."

York's eyes were narrow as he said, "Your boys best not fire the first shot."

Colman got his smirky grin going. "The first shot, Sheriff, they *already* fired . . . and *you* fired the second one."

He had indeed.

"And," Colman was saying, "I don't imagine, next time around, they'll be anybody left on the other side of the creek to say who fired the first round in the second battle of this fracas. And it's coming. It's coming."

"And I," York said bitterly, "am going."

And the sheriff strode off the beach and into the trees.

Behind him rowdy cowboys and killers were applauding him, the sound of it like gunshots echoing off the waters.

Looking very much the tomboy her late papa had raised on this ranch—hair up, plaid shirt, denims, boots—Willa Cullen stood tall on the porch, arms folded, waiting for Caleb's arrival.

For half an hour or so, she'd been stewing, pacing, before settling into this stiff, unwelcoming posture, after Bill Jackson brought her the bad news about the death of one of the three gunhands they'd taken on.

Including the particularly bad news that the sheriff had been the perpetrator of the deed.

From his expression on horseback as he drew nearer, she knew Caleb could read her mood. He looked ashen but not ashamed; he called out no greeting, didn't even nod. Just rode up and climbed off the gelding and tied it up at the hitching rail.

Of course, she didn't call to him or nod, either.

She noted that he'd left the badge pinned to his gray shirt—he *never* wore the tin when he called on her!—and he took his hat off there at the bottom of the steps, like a stranger come to call, showing respect but no familiarity.

With a nod, he said, "Willa."

Not a stranger, then.

"Caleb."

"Could we go inside and talk?"

Her instinct was *no*—he could stay down there, and not set foot even on the *steps* to this house, much less go in, not after what he'd done.

But a few ranch hands were around—Harmon and his helper in the cookhouse, old wrangler Lou Morgan who managed the barns, a few others—so maybe privacy *was* called for.

She answered his question with a nod and turned her back on him, his footsteps clunking on the stairs behind her, spurs jangling. Getting to the door before he could catch up and hold it open for her, she went in and moved immediately across the living room and deposited herself in one of the rough-hewn chairs her late father had fashioned before she was born. She sat facing a fireplace that right now was as cold as she was. Almost.

She heard him close the door—as gently as that big door could be closed. Then his footsteps came again. Slow but steady.

He came around in front of her—fireplace at his back, hat in hand, chin lowered, but not cowed—and his eyes met hers.

"I'm sorry about what happened," he said simply.

"Sorry that you killed one of my men?"

"Jackson reported to you, I assume."

"He did."

The chin lifted, the eyes remained on her. "Did he tell you that your shootist took it upon himself to fire? That he shot first? And not on your foreman's order?"

". . . He did."

"Would you have me not return fire if a man shoots at me?"

She lifted her eyebrows. "Oh, he shot specifically at you?"

Caleb thought about that, then said, "I can't rightly say. I don't think he knew *who* he was shooting at. And he hit no one, thank God. But he was in a group of armed men facing down another group of armed men, and I would say he panicked."

"Did you know who you were shooting at?"

"Yes."

"Did you panic?"

"No."

"Did you attempt to wound him?"

"No. It's a rare instance when I pull on a man and don't mean to put him down."

"And this wasn't one of those rare instances."

"No. I meant to kill him." He shook his head, just a little. "We're talking about decisions made in a moment. In a piece of a moment."

She looked at him for a while. Then: "How many men have you killed, Caleb?"

"I don't keep track."

"I believe that's a lie. I believe you do."

He hedged: "I was in the war. You don't know how many of your bullets take a life in battle."

"You fought for the North."

"I did."

"Who did you fight for today?"

"Willa . . ."

She could feel the red rising up her throat. "That rabble the Hammond witch hired on, they're mostly Arizona trash. They fought for the South, if they fought at all. My boys, those that were in the war, fought for the North."

He was shaking his head, slowly. "That's no way to look at it, Willa. . . ."

"What made you switch sides, Caleb?"

"I did not switch sides."

"What made you take sides . . . against me?"

And then she did something that she hated herself for, right then and later too: she lost control and the rage came boiling out, her cheeks hot, her eyes brimming.

She bit off the words: "Against *me*!"

". . . That's not how I look at it."

She could not stop her chin from trembling. "What else would you call it? You'd side with that Hammond woman? Over me?"

He raised a hand. "You hired gunmen, Willa. And sent your men onto your neighbor's ground to take what wasn't yours. And to burn powder if need be doing it."

"To defend what's *mine*! This *ranch*! *What my father built!*"

He took a deep breath. Let it out. "I work for the county. The *law* isn't on your side in this . . . and I am the law. That's what they pay me for, to enforce it. So in that sense I suppose I am . . . on the opposite side. I have encouraged Victoria Hammond to engage her lawyer to talk to yours and work this out in a peaceable way."

Her eyebrows climbed. "You *talked* to her?"

"I talked to her."

"And now you've *killed* for her!"

He shook his head, once. "I shot a man of questionable character who you hired to carry a gun for you, Willa. Who while on the property of the neighbor you are squabbling with . . ."

"*Squabbling!*"

". . . fired his gun in the direction of that neighbor's hired men, and might easily've incited wholesale slaughter if I didn't wade in."

Her upper lip curled. "You waded in by killing him."

A single nod. "I did."

His expression was as cold as her cheeks felt hot.

"You need to handle this in a peaceful way," he told her. "A legal way. Or else I have to quit my job and be just another gun you hired on. Maybe you'd rather I took that San Diego position with Pinkerton's. They wrote me just last month—I'm still wanted."

Her smile had little to do with the usual reasons for smiling. "You should be happy *somebody* still wants you. Go! Quit! Run off to your precious San Diego and big-city ways! See if I care." The childishness of those last words embarrassed her, and she looked away.

He leaned in and put a hand on her shoulder, his voice softening. "I don't want to leave. I don't want to leave Trinidad and I sure as hell don't want to leave you."

She swallowed. She couldn't look at him. Tears were flowing now and she hated herself for them. Hated herself!

"The world's changing, Willa. You have a chance to sell the Bar-O after that cripplin' winter made a shambles of it."

"Sell! She's offering pennies!"

"Just hold on. Think about it. I'm going to be making

right handsome money and they're even *giving* me that house. I'm not just county sheriff now, I'm town marshal. You don't need to fight this war. You love this place. I'm partial to it myself. But your father is gone. The cattle business is a mess. You've been after me for . . . how long? To put roots down in Trinidad. To marry you and settle here. Well, I'm willing to."

That snapped her out of it. No tears, but plenty of rage, a rage turned cold now.

She shoved him away, hard, and he stumbled back into the stone hearth. On her feet, she said, "Don't do me any damn favors, Caleb York!"

Hands came up in surrender. "That came out poorly. . . ."

"No, it was *exactly* what you think, *exactly* what you feel. But there's a favor you can do me—*get the hell out*!"

He swallowed, nodded, stuffed his hat on his head, and rounded the seating area, then walked quickly across the room, his spurs chasing him, and out the door. She almost ran, following him.

From the top of the steps, she saw him get up on the gray horse.

"At least I know where you stand!" she yelled.

Then, after he was gone, she said softly, "At least I know where you stand," and headed back inside, in no hurry.

Raven-haired Rita Filley, the queen of the Victory Saloon—her full-breasted, otherwise slender shape nicely accommodated by a blue-and-gray satin gown—surveyed her kingdom.

Her saloon was Trinidad's golden eyesore, though when the Sante Fe spur came in that would undoubtedly change. For now, the Victory served the town's population of three-hundred-some just fine, with plenty of trade coming from cowhands and others affiliated with the ranches in San Miguel County. And as for the railroad spur, she was confident her establishment, one of the finest of its kind in the Southwest, would fare well with whatever competition might come.

Running the biggest, fanciest watering hole in a boom town wouldn't be bad at all.

From the towering embossed steel ceiling with its kerosene-lamp chandeliers to gold-and-black brocaded walls ridden decoratively by saddles and spurs, the Victory was a palace of gambling and drink. Witness the gleaming oaken bar with its bow-tie-sporting bartenders, in back of whom nestled bottle upon bottle of bourbon along room-expanding mirrors. Cowboys and clerks lined up at the bar, with its hanging towels ready to remove foam from mustaches and a brass foot rail interrupted by occasional spittoons for the deposit of tobacco juice.

Mostly, though, the Victory was a casino, complete with dice, roulette, chuck-a-luck, and wheel of fortune. At the far end on a platform, a piano player contributed lively honky-tonk for a tiny dance floor, where grimy cowboys pawed powdered dance hall girls, but didn't get very far, not since Rita shut down the foofaraw house upstairs.

Up front, opposite the bar, were the tables where customers sat drinking, a pair of gaming tables beyond that. House dealer Yancy Cole, in his standard riverboat gambler attire, dealt faro, as he often did. At the other table, Caleb York and several City Council members were playing stud poker without a house dealer, as was their wont, and with no cut to the Victory either—a harmless payoff to the city fathers. These tables were positioned near the stairway to the second floor, which had been remodeled strictly into Rita's private quarters.

Rita had never imagined this life for herself. She'd grown up in Houston, where she'd done the books for her father's modest blacksmith shop. On her papa's death, her sister, Lola, inherited the smithy, which she sold, then came to Trinidad and opened the Victory in partnership with the notorious Sheriff Harry Gauge. That had left Rita in Houston to eke out an existence as a waitress in bars and cantinas. Lola had promised to send for her little sis, but months passed without that happening.

That Rita might inherit a business so fine and profitable as the Victory had come as a surprise. But following as it had upon her sister Lola's tragic murder at Gauge's hands was a shock. Not long before her death, Lola had written her about Caleb York and it was clear her older sister had an interest in the man.

And now the younger sister did.

York had shown plenty of interest in Rita, too, but not the marrying kind, or even the one-woman variety that Willa Cullen had inspired in the man, which fed marriage rumors around town. What Rita and York had was more a friendship, the kind that included trips upstairs to her private quarters that sometimes lasted overnight.

Those nights had tended to come when York and the Cullen girl had fallen out over something or other, which had occurred several times, if not often enough for the saloon owner to think one of these interludes might turn into a concerto.

Tonight something was different with Caleb. For one thing, he'd already been drinking when he came around.

He was not a man to drink heavily. She'd even queried about his caution with drink.

"Is it something that was a problem once?" she'd asked him upstairs, a while back. "Something you had to get shy of?"

"No. I like a drink. But it's like smoking."

Smoking he also avoided, only rarely rolling one or lighting up a cigar. Not never. Yet rare.

"How is it like smoking?" she asked.

"Smokers whose pouch runs empty—or are in circumstances where they shouldn't partake, like on a stagecoach with ladies present—can get nervous-like. Get the shakes, the way drinking men do, if they can't lay hands on the stuff."

"Some feel it's a price to pay for the enjoyment."

"They aren't men with my reputation. They aren't in my line of work. I need to be steady of eye and hand, Rita, if I aim to stay alive."

But right now, York—who almost always won at poker and when he didn't seemed at least easily able to break even—was losing. Not hand over fist, but getting money taken by the likes of Mayor Hardy, banker Burnell, druggist Davis, and even Harris, mediocre players all.

She had strolled over a couple of times and perceived the problem. He was betting recklessly—not betting big, just not paying attention. Few men she'd ever known had the focus of the tall legend that was Caleb York. Right now the only thing legendary about him was the way he seemed able to put away whiskey without falling off that chair.

The game broke up just after midnight, but Caleb was

still sitting there, shuffling the cards. That he was able to do so after all that drink was impressive, but after a time he stopped shuffling and just sat and stared.

She took the chair next to him. "Caleb, why don't you come upstairs with me?"

His eyes went to her. He smiled. "Best offer I had all night."

He got up and she took his arm, just to be sure, and he took the rail with one hand and let her guide him by holding on to him at right. She was impressed by how steady he seemed.

She walked him to her bathroom—she had indoor plumbing (the customers got the privies out back)—and he stumbled in, and when the door closed, it sounded like a horse relieving himself in there.

Then, in the bedroom of her suite, with furnishings she'd had shipped in from Denver, she helped him out of his coat, gun belt, and boots, and onto the big brass canopied bed with satin spread, flounces, and pillows. He was already half asleep, and an anomaly in this determinedly feminine room with its walnut furnishings, velvet curtains, and loomed rugs with flowery designs.

The bed was big enough for two and she got undressed and put on her nightgown and curled up beside him. He smelled like whiskey. Generally, he smelled bad.

But here he was, and she had him all to herself.

And yet she had heard the rumors about the conflict between Victoria Hammond and Willa Cullen. Somehow that played into this. Was he in this condition, and here in her bedroom, because things were again amiss between him and Willa?

She didn't care. She just didn't care. She had him. And

this time she would keep him. She fell asleep, filled with an oddly hysterical joy.

Then in the middle of the night, he spoke in his sleep, dreaming.

One word.

"Willa," he said.

With whom Rita suddenly had something in common, too, because she was another strong woman in tears.

CHAPTER TEN

Deputy Sheriff Jonathan P. Tulley had never been versed in the notion of three meals a day, till of late.

Back in his prospecting days, the staples of his diet had been coffee, hardtack, and jerky. And since he'd come to Trinidad two years or more ago, when he was living under the boardwalk, he'd settled for what scraps he could wangle from back of the café and the hotel restaurant.

After he got himself cleaned up and dried out, thanks to Caleb York, Tulley had got that job sweeping out and doing general chores and such at the livery stable, where blacksmith Clem Hansen shared his stew and chili beans and such like, midday, which was generally enough to keep a skinny creature like Tulley going. And did that Clem make a mean cornbread! The smoke of it cooking had darn near drowned out the manure smell.

But these here days, Tulley was a working man, with a monthly paycheck and clean clothes, and a once-a-month customer at the bathhouse behind the mayor's barbershop, where he also got his whiskers and what growth remained on top of his skull tended to. Even got splashed with bay rum, and the barbering mayor used some kind of daubing stick on wherever Tulley got nicked.

These things the deputy settled up for out of his pay, and happy to; but other things were what Caleb York called "perquisites." The main one of these was the three meals a day Tulley partook of, which were the cause of the small paunch he was growing that was challenging the button at the front of his store-bought britches.

The café donated his breakfast, eggs, and taters and a biscuit or sometimes oatmeal and cornbread (not as good as Clem's, however). This privilege came because the folks running the place was paid for serving up food for the jailhouse prisoners, which San Miguel County didn't have any of right now. Tulley would partake of that fare, in such cases. Visitors to the calaboose only et twice a day, though—coffee in the morning was all they got. Maybe some hardtack, if they had the teeth for it.

The restaurant at the hotel let Tulley have a plate of things they had left at closing, which tallied with when he started his nightly rounds. The dining room was closed and they let him sit in that fancy space all by hisself, chowing down on beef and more taters and even sometimes pie. This was fare he was used to, as he'd often sampled their menu in his under-the-boardwalk days, taking potluck out of the refuse can. The hotel folk was always nice to him back then, letting him sit on the rear stoop and just help himself. They even thanked him— said it helped keep the dogs away.

So that was breakfast and supper. And in between was lunch over to the Victory. The saloon served up free cold cuts to drinking men, also yellow cheese, rye bread, celery stalks, pretzels, peanuts, smoked herring, and dill pickles, all good and salty, to make a body good and thirsty. Now in Tulley's case, being on the wagon as he was, "drink" only meant coffee or maybe sarsaparilla, but Miss Rita didn't charge him nothing for either of them.

This perquisite stuff weren't a'tall bad, he told himself.

Things were slow at the Victory, even for a weekday, as Tulley sat at one of the tables opposite the bar, tended to only by Hub Wainright currently. Just a handful of cowboys was on hand, though a good share of clerks and such on their lunch hours were tossin' back a beer or two with their free lunch.

The deputy sat alone, just nibbling at the cold cuts and cheese, barely chomping on the celery, hardly tasting the dill pickle, even if it did make his eyes water.

Caleb York had not been in to work today.

Not yet. The desk in the office had sat empty all morning. Tulley hadn't got worried till about ten. The sheriff often took his time coming in, particularly when they didn't have any guests checked in to the "Hoosegow Hotel." Like now.

For a man who didn't talk much, Caleb York had a sociable side. He would stop in at stores and see how folks was doing, find out if any trouble were afoot. Stop by businesses like the bank and the undertaker's, maybe stick his head in at the *Enterprise* newspaper, if he was irritated with the editor at the time.

But Tulley had stopped in at most of those places himself today, asking after the sheriff, and nobody said they'd seen him. And Tulley himself hadn't seen him since yesterday afternoon, when his boss said he was riding out to see the Hammond woman.

Now, he had a way with the ladies, Caleb York did, and Tulley had heard tell the Hammond woman was a fine figure of a handsome female of the species, which could mean that was where the randy, badge-wearing so-and-so may well have spent the night.

But it wasn't likely he'd wound up at the hotel, and his room there, because Wilson, the chinless clerk, said he hadn't seen the sheriff, not last evening nor this morning. And the stairs were right next to the check-in desk.

Of course, Miss Willa lived out that general direction, and that was probably the answer. Several times in recent weeks, Caleb York had stayed out to the Bar-O till dawn, or anyway so Tulley figured (not wanting to pry). So probably nothing to worry about.

Probably.

Problem was, Caleb York lived an eventful kind of life, and Tulley could not stop his imagination from bucking like a bronco. Never mind the tales they told about the sheriff in his Wells Fargo days, or what they wrote about in the dime novels—that man attracted trouble like Tulley had attracted fleas under the boardwalk. Since Caleb York rode in town a stranger, the deputy had been at that man's side, fighting outlaws and other no-goods, enough times to challenge *any* gun-fighting lawman's reputation—and all in under a year!

Tulley wouldn't have believed half of it if he hadn't suffered through most of it.

Still, it weren't like the man couldn't handle hisself. Nothing to worry about.

Tulley picked up a piece of pickled herring and tossed it in his pie hole and chewed, then swallowed. Not a thing to worry about. Nossir.

Then he noticed Miss Rita, leaning against the bar like just another cowboy, watching him. This time of day she rarely was seen in one of them fancy gowns. Wearing no face paint whatsoever, she was covered up, neck to floor, in a light blue blouse with puffy sleeves and a black walking skirt.

His mouth full of yellow cheese, Tulley smiled and

nodded to the proprietess, and she came over, walking nice and easy, smiling the same way. Minus the cheese.

Miss Rita pulled a chair out and sat herself down. In that silky voice of hers, she said, "I bet you're wondering what's become of Caleb York."

Tulley felt his face go red. Lunch wasn't the only reason he'd come, and in fact he was in here an hour earlier than was typical. Caleb York having a way with the ladies included Miss Rita Filley, and the sheriff had spent more than one night upstairs in the quarters where this beauteous saloon gal lay herself down at night.

But that hadn't happened for a while, not since Caleb York and Miss Willa let word out they was preparing to wed. The sheriff had standards and morals and such, and that was among the virtues Jonathan P. Tulley admired in the man, near as much as he admired the way Caleb York could put bad men in the ground.

She folded her hands, which had long, tapering fingers, and leaned forward, confidential-like.

"Caleb's fine, Mr. Tulley," she said.

Tulley let out a sigh that began at the tips of the toes of his boots. "I am right glad to hear that, Miss Rita. Right glad."

"He's upstairs now, as it happens," she said, with a nod in that direction. "Sleeping it off."

The deputy frowned at her in puzzlement. "Sleepin' *what* off?"

That seemed to amuse her. "I would think you, of *all* people, would know what it means to sleep it off, Mr. Tulley."

His frown dug deeper. "Ye shorely cannot mean that the sheriff drank hisself under the table."

She pointed past the deputy. "No, he stayed upright in a chair at that table right there . . . where he was playing with the mayor and a few others. He was losing, by the way."

Tulley cocked his head. "Losin' what?"

"Money. At poker."

He reared back a tad. "I suppose that happens to the best of 'em."

Her eyebrows rose. "Caleb York lose to the likes of Clem Davis and Newt Harris? And banker Burnell?"

Tulley thought about it. "Probably jes' gettin' their guard down, 'fore he pounced."

Rita smirked. "If by 'pounced' you mean losing several hundred dollars to them, then yes. He sat there drinking and losing all evening, until I walked him upstairs and he flopped on the bed, asleep or passed out. Either way, he's *still* out."

The deputy was shaking his head. "Jes' had hisself a bad night."

She bobbed her head toward the bar. "It's been slow here, but a few cowpokes stopped by. Funny how after getting a few beers in 'em, those boys do talk. Worse than a bunch of gossiping old women."

"Ain't they, though—they go on 'bout anythin' tickler?"

She nodded, her pretty dark eyes half-lidded now. "You've heard the rumors about hired guns signing on with both Willa Cullen and the Hammond woman?"

He nodded back, forcefully. "I have. I be the very one tol' the sheriff! That's why he headed out to the Circle G yesterdee."

She sighed, and there was no sign of amusement in that pretty face now. "That goes along with what I heard from those cowhands. Talk is, small armies from both camps were lined up yesterday along the opposite banks of Sugar Creek . . . and that one of the Bar-O riders was shot and killed."

"Oh my."

"Someone called Clements, a gunfighter."

Tulley grunted. "Not *much* of a one, t'would seem."

"Well, he *was* up against the best."

"Oh *my!*" Tulley squinted at her. "*Caleb York* shot one of Miz Cullen's hirelings! Why would he *do* such a thing?"

"Apparently Clements shot first."

". . . That'd do it." Tulley mulled some. "So after that sad state of affairs, the legend sits down and punishes hisself, losin' to his lessers, and then gets soused to the gills like there weren't no t'morrow."

Her eyes were wide now. "Well, there *is* a tomorrow, and this is it—but he still hasn't come down."

The deputy pushed away his plate, which was empty, and got to his feet. "Wal, *some* fool's got to be the law in Trinidad till he gets hisself up and around."

Tulley started to stalk out, but reaching the batwing doors, he paused and looked back at the lovely saloon owner. "You inform that Caleb York that Jonathan P. Tulley was in! That I will be at my post. You tell him so!"

She smiled gently. "I will, Deputy. I will."

Back inside the adobe jailhouse, Tulley stewed and paced, and paced and stewed. His general pattern in the afternoon was to take a nap in one of the cells—he lived out of the kind of beat-up old suitcase cowboys called a cooster, which he would transport to whatever accommodations might be free in the little cellblock. He preferred the lockup right off the office, and mostly used that as his casa, but sometimes Caleb York had a prisoner in-house who he wanted to keep a close eye on.

Having somewhere warm to sleep with a roof over his head, other than hay in a stall over at the livery, was a perquisite Tulley quite relished. The cots were right comfortable, and most afternoons he fell asleep as soon as he settled. Today, with his mind ajitter with worry over Caleb York's situation, Tulley took an endless near three minutes of tossing and turning before nodding off.

Normally Caleb York would have been in and out of the office enough for Tulley to get roused at some point. But today—or tonight, more like—the deputy didn't wake till moonlight was coming through the high barred window. He got himself up, went out and poured some coffee and drank it down. The clock on the wall high up behind the sheriff's desk said eleven-fifteen—Judas Priest, how long had Tulley been sawing logs, anyway?

He'd slept through his chores, such as sweeping out and mopping up as needed. No time for that before starting up his evening rounds, which he decided to tend to.

Soon he was heading down the boardwalk, shotgun in hand. Things was typically deserted, this time of night, save for the Victory Saloon, where the windows were letting out light like the place was burning up.

He pushed through the batwings and found Hell's half acre hopping. Some of the same cowhands and clerks were back, or were maybe still there, plus more of both breeds, keeping the dice, roulette, chuck-a-luck, and wheel of fortune stations bustling. The piano player was pounding out hurdy-gurdy-type tunes while grubby cowpokes and fancy gals cuddled upright—just because no rental brides was taking them temporary grooms upstairs no more didn't mean some hanky-panky weren't still being arranged.

Yancy Cole was dealing faro again, and Caleb York was back playing poker with the city fathers, looking to win back what they took from him the night before, t'would seem. The sheriff's black frock coat looked rumpled and his hat was shoved back on his head. He could have used a shave. At his elbow was a glass of brown liquid that was likely whiskey. He had a few piles of chips in front of him, whereas several of his friendly opponents had assembled a number of towers of such chips, blue, red, orange, and white.

The mayor was shuffling, so Tulley took that moment to sidle up to Caleb York.

"Sheriff," he said.

"Deputy." Not looking at Tulley.

"Ye be missed today."

"Any trouble?"

"No! No, sir. Quiet. Like a Sunday service, minus the preacher jawin'."

"Good."

Cards were being dealt now. It was a five-card draw game. Dealer's choice.

Tulley cleared his throat. "Word is they was trouble out to Sugar Crick."

"Some."

"You have to shoot a man?"

"Yes."

"Pulled on you, did he?"

"He pulled. Why I shot him."

"One of Miss Willa's guntoters, was it?"

"Yes. They were on Hammond land. Tulley, I'm playing cards."

"So I see."

"Pull up a chair or find somewhere else to be."

"You know I don't indulge in games of chance, Caleb York."

"I do know. And kibitzers ain't allowed. Which leaves you one choice."

Tulley knew what choice that was. He shuffled over to the bar. Miss Rita, in a green gown trimmed white, came up and said, "He's losing even worse tonight. At his request, I've been feeding him straight whiskey and poker chips all evening. Tin box under the bar has five IOUs of his in it."

"Caleb York's got the money."

"I know he does. But Tulley, I'm worried. I never saw him like this."

"Nor I."

She told bartender Hub Wainwright to get Tulley a sarsaparilla, and left the deputy at the bar amongst the others bellied up there, and proceeded to thread through the customers, spreading smiles and nods.

Tulley had just finished his glass of the sweet soda water when across the room Caleb York pushed his chair away from the table and stood, not terribly steady about it. No chips were in front of him. He made an awkward trip over to the bar where Miss Rita was talking to Hub.

Conversation ensued but didn't last long, and Caleb York hustled out, damn near losing his balance doing so.

Tulley got up and went over to the saloon gal and didn't even have to ask what it was about. She just started right in.

"I cut him off," she said, looking a little pale. "No more money, no more whiskey."

"He's got money in the safe and whiskey in a desk drawer."

"He said as much to me," she told the deputy. "Said he'd be back in a flash."

"On his hands and knees, more like. He's so drunk he couldn't hit the ground with his hat in three throws."

Her expression screamed worry. "Better follow him, Mr. Tulley. If he's headed back to the jail, maybe you can talk sense to him."

Tulley felt kind of honored by that. It had been many

years since anyone had suggested to Tulley that he might be the right person to talk sense to anyone.

Shotgun stock tight in his left hand, Tulley exited the saloon into a moon-swept night and an empty street. *Almost* empty—ahead on the boardwalk, Caleb York was halfway up the next block, obviously on his way back to the jail. He was not moving fast. In fact, he was weaving.

That may have saved his life.

Because when the shot cracked the emptiness like small sudden thunder—coming from across the street, around the corner, orange muzzle flame making a brief brightness in the dark—the sheriff had made a moving target of himself by almost losing his balance.

Tulley, already running toward the danger, saw Caleb York sober up just long enough to draw his .44 and duck backward into the recession of a storefront's entryway. Tulley—his footfall making the boards beneath creak and groan—yelled, "Stay put, Sheriff! Stay put!"

The deputy ran into the street and across, shotgun primed for action, but when he got to the corner and peeked around, and then stepped out, nothing was waiting but the stench of gunpowder. Beyond were the handful of residences back there. Not a light in any window, not even second floor. Then he heard hoofbeats that quickly receded, and figured the trouble was leaving of its own accord.

Best check and make sure the sheriff hadn't been hit.

He did so, finding Caleb York huddled against the doorway of the pharmacy with his .44 in a shaking fist.

"He hightailed, Sheriff," Tulley said, slipping an arm around his friend's shoulder. "Ye ain't hit, is ye?"

"No . . . no . . ."

"You reckon ye had enough cards and whiskey to suit you for a night?"

The sheriff nodded. His body relaxed. He seemed almost asleep, his eyelids at half-mast.

Tulley said, "Bein' as ye is already three sheets to the wind, let's get ye 'tween some nice *clean* sheets over to the hotel."

Getting no argument, Tulley slipped his right arm around Caleb York's waist, keeping the shotgun ready in his left fist, and walked him to the Trinidad House. The going was slow, with Tulley looking every which way in case the shooter doubled back; but they made it.

Wilson, the desk clerk, got Tulley the room key and even helped him half-drag their charge up the stairs and down the hall and to the sheriff's door. Once inside, with a lamp lit low, they took off the now-unconscious man's coat—his hat had been lost along the way—and his gun belt and boots, then slung him into the bed and got the covers over him.

Not an experienced hotel guest himself, Tulley knew nothing of tipping, and yet he appreciated what Wilson helped him do so much he dug a quarter eagle out of his pants and handed it over.

Wilson, who seemed to appreciate that, left and Caleb York began to snore.

Tulley shook his head. He felt sympathy, having been on more benders in a lifetime than a man should have been able to survive. But he thought he'd never see such a thing out of Caleb York, and it did disappoint him. In another sense, though, he didn't mind seeing this man was a human after all.

Someone burst in the room and Tulley jerked the shotgun up and damn near shot a hole in Miss Rita.

He didn't, though, and if she realized she'd almost been subject of a tragedy, she didn't show it none. She just shut the door behind her, looking like the damnedest apparition standing there with her bosom heaving in that silk-and-satin green thing—the kind of dress that seemed befitting in a saloon but just plain strange anywheres else.

She leaned over the bed and she stroked the snoring man's face, like he was a child of hers with a fever.

"Someone said a shot was fired," she said, her eyes wide and almost accusative. "Someone else said they saw you hauling Caleb over here. What happened?"

Tulley told her.

She stood straight, but them creamy mounds was still heaving. Mercy sakes.

"I'll be back," she said. "Meantime, you stand guard."

"I was aimin' to sit. On a chair? In the hall?"

"That's fine," she said.

And that's what he was doing, shotgun in his lap, when she returned in the light blue shirt and black riding skirt and boots. She had a small revolver in hand.

Tulley was blocking the door, so he stood and moved the chair for her to go into the room. She paused before she did, saying, "That window on the street could give someone access."

"Ye mean they could climb up and crawl in?"

"Exactly what I mean. I'll sit at the foot of his bed and you stay out here. Maybe by morning he'll have come to his senses."

"One can only hope. . . . Ye know how to use that peashooter, Miss Rita?"

She nodded. "A man in Houston tried to force his way on me once and I shot him."

"Kill him?"

"I did."

"How many shots?"

"Just the one." She touched her forehead near the bridge of her nose.

Then she slipped inside the room.

What a female, Tulley thought, smiling to himself, as he sat back down and cradled the shotgun like a precious child.

CHAPTER ELEVEN

While hardly a teetotaler, Caleb York was not what you'd call a hard-drinking man. He could have tallied up on his fingers the times he'd been hung over in his life, with digits to spare.

The condition had afflicted him often enough, however, for him to recognize the signs: feeling tired however much sleep he'd had, a bilious stomach, and a pounding headache, not helped by the midmorning sun. That had driven York from his usual window seat in the Trinidad House Hotel's dining room to this one in a far corner.

That window seat had been "usual" in the sense that when he took supper here (which was frequent) that spot with a view onto the street was reserved for him. And taking breakfast at the hotel was not at all usual, as he took advantage of the arrangement with the town café to feed prisoners at the jail to get himself a free morning meal, almost every day.

Not this one.

Coming down the steps in the clothes he'd slept in, and making it into the dining room, was as major an expedition as he cared to embark upon right now, particularly with that morning sun painting the world out there a painful yellow.

So he was settled, with his back to the corner where the far walls met (expanding his expedition but in an acceptable manner) so he could sit with his back unexposed. After all, he had dreamt last night of being shot at and he'd woken with a dizzy sense that maybe that had not been a nightmare at all.

Choosing the hotel dining room this morning also had to do with the superior fare—he could get a nice big steak of the best quality, and despite his lingering nausea, a slab of rare dead beef with some eggs was what had once been recommended to him as a hangover cure of sorts by a doctor. That the doctor in question was named Holliday only served to lend the prescription verity.

The food had not yet arrived but he was already on his second cup of coffee, attempting to quench what seemed to him a surprising thirst considering how much liquid he'd tossed down over the past—damn, *two days* was it?

And had he dreamed, too, of losing hundreds of dollars to those amateurs on the City Council?

At half-past ten, the dining room was otherwise empty—too late for breakfast, too early for lunch—but a frantic pair came rushing in nonetheless, as if desperate to find seating.

In reality, they were looking to see where York might be seated: Rita Filley, mussed but lovely in a shirt and riding dress, her revolver in hand, and Tulley, shotgun in his hand, store-bought clothes looking so rumpled the old boy might have slept under the boardwalk last night, like the not-so-good-old-days.

Of course, York knew damn well where Tulley had spent the previous night, and Rita as well. The sheriff had woken to find the latter in a chair, asleep, facing the window, a revolver in her lap; and York had slipped around the former, asleep in a chair in front of the hotel room door, shotgun cradled, as if the deputy were in the Land of Nod with a lovely wench he was wooing.

Well, anybody can dream.

They charged over and fixed themselves side by side before him, looking down with alarm and accusation.

"Good morning," York managed to say, between sips of coffee.

"Thank God," Rita said. "We didn't know *where* you'd gone off to!"

"Caleb York," Tulley said, trembling, "ye put a right *scare* in the two of us!"

York winced and raised a hand. "No need to shout," he said gently. "Pull up a chair. Both of you."

They did.

"Coffee?" he asked them. Place settings with cups were before them, and the waiter had left York a steaming pot of Arbuckle's.

"No thank ye," Tulley said. "I prefer my own."

York and Rita exchanged raised-eyebrow looks, but let the opinion stand.

Then York said, "I dreamed someone shot at me last night."

"Tweren't no dream," Tulley said.

York grunted, and it hurt. "Suspected as much."

"Ye got yore gun out of its scabbard," his deputy said, "but that be about all. Had sense enough to duck in a doorway, anyways."

"Did you see who, Tulley?"

"No. Come from across the street. Feller lit out like his

tail was afire. Heard his horse sweepin' him off to hell and gone. Pardon the language, Miss Rita."

York looked from one to the other. "And you two stood guard on me? All night?"

Rita's nod was barely perceptible. Tulley's was so enthusiastic York could barely watch, the deputy adding, "Sat, not stood. And might be dropped off a second or two."

The Victory's hostess, frowning in thought, asked, "Who would want you dead, Caleb?"

"It's a long list." He sipped. "Going back fifteen years, leastways."

She leaned forward. Even with her hair a tangle, and not a lick of face paint, she was a lovely, dark-eyed creature, almost enough to make a man not want to crawl off somewhere and die.

"Caleb," she said quietly, "let me amend that—who would want you dead right *now*?"

He thought about it. That took effort, as the throbbing headache just didn't want to make room.

"Rita," he said, "best candidate would be one of Willa's hired guns. You've heard about them?"

She nodded. "Cowboys like to talk almost as much as they like to drink. And word's around you shot and killed one of the Circle G riders."

He nodded back. "Wes Hardin's cousin."

Tulley's eyes popped. "Heaven's bells! Now you got John Wesley Hardin out to get ye!"

York smiled, just a little. Bigger would have hurt.

"I doubt that," he said. "News doesn't travel *that* fast. Anyway, Hardin doesn't give a damn about anybody but himself, and he prefers facing down men slower and less dangerous."

Rita was frowning. "I can't imagine Willa Cullen would . . . no, that's out of the question."

"She wouldn't," York said confidently. "We've had a . . . falling-out, it's true. But, no. Somebody in her crew who wanted to get back at me—one of the other guns—maybe."

Rita's chin lifted. "Victoria Hammond hired on guns, too. Maybe one of them would want you out of the picture."

"That makes more sense, only . . ."

"Only?"

"I was on her side of the creek. When I fired across and killed that man."

"On her side of the creek? On her side of the war, you mean!"

"I'm on the *county's* side, Rita. The law's side."

She shook her head slowly. "But that's not how Willa sees it, I would guess."

"No," he admitted. "It's not."

His food came, the steak sizzling. When the waiter had left, York summoned a smile.

"Would you two be willin' to do me another favor? One apiece?"

Tulley and Rita just listened.

"Rita," York said, "go back to the Victory and keep your eyes and ears open. Either Tulley or I will be by from time to time to see what, if anything, you've picked up."

"All right," she said. "And if it's urgent . . . ?"

"I'll likely be at my office. I need to recover a bit before I take any kind of action."

"And," Tulley advised, "what *kinder* action needs takin'."

"Truer words," York said with a smile that came more

easy now. "Deputy, go get yourself some sleep in your favorite cell. I imagine you only caught a few hours last night. I'll rouse you if you're needed."

Tulley's eyes narrowed. "Anything else, Caleb York?"

"Yes. You two let me try to eat this dead animal in peace. I might get it down, but it may come up again, and that won't be pretty."

They rose to go, but York found himself somehow rising, too. He reached a hand out and touched Rita's cheek, momentarily, and her eyes got big and wet.

York looked at her, then at Tulley.

"No drunken son of a bitch," he said, "ever had better friends."

Tulley's smile was endless, but Rita's smile was tight and her chin was crinkled. She swallowed and was gone, Tulley trailing.

It did not occur to York that calling her a friend might not strike her as enough.

He ate slowly, chewing the beef thoroughly before sending it down his gullet, washing everything down with hot coffee. When he had finished, he pushed the plate away and just sat there, letting his stomach deal with the problem.

The dishes had been cleared away and York was considering whether to risk getting to his feet again when another individual entered the dining room. By now it was after eleven o'clock and those taking an early lunch would be filtering in. First of these was a familiar face.

White-haired, white-mustached Raymond Parker was about as distinguished-looking a character as anyone might ever hope to encounter in Trinidad, New Mexico. In his double-breasted gray-trimmed-black Newmarket coat, lighter gray waistcoat, and darker gray trousers, the fiftyish businessman cut an impressive citified figure, modified by that Western touch of a gray Stetson.

Doffing that hat, Parker beamed as he spotted York in his quiet corner, and came quickly over. "May I join you?"

"Please."

The businessman appraised the sheriff carefully. "You look pale, man. Are you ill?"

"Nothing catching."

One eyebrow went up. "Caleb York—unshaven, red eyed, with the general aspect of a kicked hound." Parker reached in his pocket for his polished steel cigar case. "If I didn't know you better, I'd say you were hung over."

Parker was about to open the case when York said, "If you don't put that thing away, I'll have to kill you."

The laugh that came was loud enough to make York wince again. "So you *are* hung over. What's the occasion? This mess with the Bar-O and Circle G?"

York nodded.

Parker tucked the case away in a side coat pocket and said, "So it's true you shot a man. One of the gunfighters imported from Las Vegas."

York nodded again, then added, "And last night someone took a shot at me."

"Must have sobered you up."

"For a few seconds. But now I'm making staying sober a general policy."

"Not a bad one at that." Parker's humorous demeanor faded and he seemed almost grave when he said, "Something has to be done about this budding range war."

"I'm trying."

"By shooting and killing a man?"

York explained the situation, briefly.

"There's still time to shut this thing down," Parker

said. "And we *need* to. Not just because we're good citizens, either."

"Isn't that enough?"

Parker flipped a hand. "Should be. But turning Trinidad from a bump in the road to a town and then a city will take more than good citizens. And more brains than bullets . . . meaning no offense."

"I like to think I have access to both."

"You do. Didn't mean to imply otherwise." Parker poured himself some coffee; it was still hot, or anyway hot enough. "The Santa Fe had to hold up starting work on the spur because of the blizzards, as you know. But there is still time for them to change their mind."

"Why would they?"

"Well," the businessman said, and shrugged, "if you were the Santa Fe Railroad, would you want to bring in teams to lay track in the middle of the equivalent of the Lincoln County War?"

Casual as the words were delivered, they came as a slap.

"No," York said.

Parker leaned in confidentially. "Which would make that land you own, and the train station I have contracted to build upon that land, about as valuable as Confederate money."

"I suppose that's true."

He threw a hand in the air. "Oh, it's true, all right. Caleb, Trinidad will wither away and die without the railroad. And you'll have a handsome chunk of worthless property on the outskirts of a ghost town."

York shifted in his chair; it took effort. "Raymond, I have talked to Willa. She's armed and ready to fight with Victoria Hammond. Hell, she's ready to fight with me."

Parker's head tilted to one side. "If you'll forgive my

intruding into personal territory . . . that wouldn't be another reason for this hangover, would it?"

York ignored that. "The Hammond woman isn't helping any. She lied to me, or anyway dissembled. She indicated she wanted me to help convince Willa to sell the Bar-O, but her offer to Willa was insulting. Pennies per acre."

Parker's eyes were narrowed. "How is it that Victoria Hammond is even on speaking terms with you, Caleb? You killed her son. I would think she would, if anything, be plotting your downfall."

"Perhaps she is. But she presents herself as a practical woman, and paints her son as a troubled soul who met a sad fate that was likely inevitable."

Parker was shaking his head. "A parent losing a child is rarely practical. And I know some things about her that you don't."

"Yeah?"

"Yes. I had her looked into by your friends the Pinkertons. And I asked friendly rivals of mine, as well . . . about her and her late husband, whose reputation as an unprincipled bastard I was already well-acquainted with. Andrew Hammond was a swindler and a cheat, and my guess is his wife is no better. It's likely their moving south was merely to make rustling in Mexico more convenient, because almost certainly that is how she intends to restock and expand the Circle G herd."

"That's opinion. What facts did you come up with?"

Parker leaned back, arms folded. "The Hammond ranch in Colorado is tottering, after the Big Die-Up, and their bank is facing ruin. Victoria Hammond seems to be trying to stave off outright failure by snatching up as much land in this part of the world as she can, and as much surviving cattle. The paltry offer to Miss Cullen from Mrs. Hammond may in part be all Lady Victoria can afford. If this range war develops, and Willa has to make peace by way of selling out, any offer she takes for the Bar-O should definitely be in cash."

York raised a palm. "Raymond, I hold no sway over Willa now. And the badge I'm hired to wear puts me squarely on the Hammond side of Sugar Creek. What would you have me do?"

Parker's voice was low, confidential, even though the chamber was largely empty of anyone but them. "We need to play for time. If you'll keep this powder keg from blowing up in the faces of all concerned, I can finish my work in Denver."

"What work?"

"I'm leaving on the stage today to catch the train at Las Vegas. Back in Denver I have put together a consortium of investors to buy up Mexican cattle—not just *steal* it—so that I can offer Willa Cullen my help in restocking the Bar-O. It will require her letting me back in as a partner, but it will save the ranch and her holdings."

York was slowly nodding. "She would go along with that, I think. Have you talked to her?"

"Not yet. It's not solid. When I get back, with a deal, then I will approach Willa. But even so, that doesn't solve her water rights problem."

York grunted. "What does?"

"Stalling for time might. Once I have my investors, and Willa says yes to me as a partner, I will bring in the best lawyers in the Southwest and we will shut Victoria Hammond down. My legal advisors tell me the handshake deal of the prior owners for shared water right of way is as good as a contract, and the responsibility will carry over to the new owner—Victoria Hammond—unless the deed says otherwise."

"How long will that take?"

"Not long. Not more than a week."

York let out something that wasn't quite a laugh. "Raymond, a week is an eternity when two armed camps are facing each other over a narrow strip of water. And how long can cattle go without water?"

"I may have a way around that." The businessman's eyes grew shrewd. "For now, suppose you inform both sides that you will view any gunplay—any shooting, particularly any fatal shooting . . . other than by yourself, of course—as assault or murder or, hell, disturbing the peace. But shut it down!"

". . . You have a lot of confidence in one man, Raymond."

"Actually, I do. But I'm thinking you might have an easier time of it with a posse."

York's eyebrows rose. "A posse? What, of the barber and druggist and undertaker and a bunch of clerks?"

Parker's upper lip curled nastily. "No. More like hard men out of Las Vegas. Those women aren't the only ones who can hire guns." He reached into the same inside pocket where he deposited the cigar case and came back with a thick fold of cash.

"Here's fifty brownbacks," Parker told York. "That's a thousand dollars in United States currency. Twenty-dollar bills."

York took them, feeling a little dazed doing so.

"Go hire yourself a posse," Parker said, "and shut this war down."

"By declaring war on both sides?"

"One way to look at it. Have you a better idea, Caleb?"

York shook his head and pocketed the lump of cash.

Parker stood. "I'm afraid I won't be able to join you for lunch. My stage leaves at noon."

York found a smile. "That's all right. I'm still working at keeping breakfast down."

Parker laughed. "I'll wire you with any news."

"If things go to hell," York said, "I won't have to wire you. The newspapers will cover it."

The dining room still wasn't busy, although a few tables were taken by now. York sat with his elbows on the linen cloth and his hands on his chin, leaning forward in thought. Parker had left him with plenty to chew on, now that the steak was gone, in particular the notion of putting together yet another crew of gun handlers.

A boyish young man in a brown suit and limp black bow tie wandered in, looking a bit lost; he was clutching a derby in his hands. Though York did not recognize him, the boy picked the sheriff out in his quiet corner and came over quickly but carefully, threading through the mostly empty tables.

Only when the young man—twenty, perhaps?—deposited himself before York did the resemblance to Victoria Hammond come through—chiefly the large, dark eyes, and feminine lashes that would not help the boy out West.

"Caleb York?" he whispered.

"Yes. You're a Hammond, aren't you?"

The boy swallowed, nodded, clutched the hat to a suit coat that hadn't come cheap. "Yes—Pierce. My mother is Victoria."

York gestured. "Have a seat, Pierce."

He shook his head, a firm no. "My mother asked me to arrange a private meeting for her with you."

"All right. I'll ride out this afternoon, if that's acceptable."

His eyes popped. "It isn't! Can you be at the cemetery at dusk? That would be around seven."

"I can."

"Mother will be visiting my brother's grave. Making sure they did right by him, till the stone arrives."

"All right."

The boy swallowed. "She told me not to linger. Best the Hammonds not be seen talking to you at any length, Sheriff."

"Okay. Till seven, then."

The boy didn't even bother to nod before he turned and went out, even quicker than he'd come.

CHAPTER TWELVE

The cool blue touch of dusk was just threatening to darken into night as Caleb York, on the dappled gray gelding, drew near Boot Hill, the slight slope of which made its name such an exaggeration. His destination, just half a mile out of town, was to the right as he rode up, and a buckboard with a single Morgan horse was waiting on the other side of the rutted road, tied up to one of two hitching posts that served the cemetery.

Apparently Victoria Hammond had beaten him here. The buckboard suggested she wasn't alone—perhaps Pierce, her son, who'd brought York's invitation to this meeting, was with her.

But there was no sign of the woman in the neatly rowed-off collection of wooden crosses and flat grave markers, some wood, a few stone. He slowed the horse to a stop and then climbed down and tied the steed up at the other hitching post, the one near the resilient mesquite tree, whose color and shade were likely the reason this otherwise desolate spot had been chosen as the resting place for departed citizens of Trinidad, New Mexico.

Right now the sprawling tree that stood watch on this

place was just an abstract silhouette, providing no color at all, and its shade was merely one jagged shadow throwing a pool of darkness. The sky was purple, edged streaky orange at the west, and to the north scarred buttes were like towering tombstones, as if perhaps Indian gods had been buried in the sandy earth below.

Standing at the edge of this field with its crop of dead gave even a brave man like Caleb York pause.

No, not crop of dead.

Harvest.

How many men had he put here? He knew. He knew. And he wasn't proud of it, either, yet there wasn't one he wouldn't send here again.

The absence of the woman who'd summoned him began to worry him. He moved slowly through the boneyard, stepping around graves, including the fresh one that housed William Hammond, glancing from side to side.

Where was she?

This began to feel wrong. At the far east side of the cemetery was the handful of headstones of various respectable citizens, relatively new residents of this city of the dead, fieldstone and granite, shipped in from Denver.

Towering over them—well, towering was an exaggeration, he supposed—was a modest mausoleum, as mausoleums went, with the word CULLEN carved in marble above its wrought-iron door. Willa had sprung for this, and had moved her mother inside to be with her father, who had inspired in his daughter this tribute.

No one considered this inappropriate, not that York knew, at least. After all, George Cullen had made the existence of Trinidad possible. He had brought in tradesmen to occupy land he gave them to have the convenience of a town near his ranch. The man had been, in his way, in his day, the kind of cattle baron that the would-be cattle baroness could never rival.

"You won't rate anything so fine, York," a male voice said.

York looked toward the sound as Clay Colman, his Peacemaker drawn and ready, came around from behind the structure, his smile curling up into a smirk. The gun-fighting Cowboy had worn black to better blend in with the night, but the brown of his hat made the rattlesnake band stand out, and his pale, clean-shaven complexion and blue-eyed blond looks were whitish smears in the near night.

Colman's tone struck York as a little too self-satisfied: "Did you think I forgot?"

"Forgot what, Colman?"

Now an edge came in, and the blue eyes narrowed in the white blur of face. "Not what. *Who.* Do you remember, York? *Owen Burge.*"

"Bit familiar."

"*Burrell Eyler.*"

"Might I do."

Colman thrust the gun forward, his barrel accusatory. "Do you need remindin'?"

A dry wind was blowing, gentle, but enough to stir hat brims and rustle sagebrush.

"No," York said. "They were in on that stagecoach holdup. You slipped away. Well, I never had enough to really go after you."

"But you got *them,* didn't you?"

"I did. I recovered the ten thousand for Wells Fargo, too. At my five percent reward, that's five hundred more than you made."

The almost too handsome face scowled. "Shot down like dogs in the street."

"No. Like fools. They pulled on me, Colman—two men on one. Damn near as bad as back-shooting."

"*You've* shot men in the back."

"I have," York admitted. "When they were fleeing and I didn't feel like running after them."

The sounds were simultaneous—somebody coming up behind him at the far left, somebody else behind him at the far right. Slow, trying not to be heard, but coming. Whoever they were, they'd either tucked themselves behind the mesquite or found one of the larger grave markers to skulk behind.

But that didn't matter.

What mattered was this had just turned into three to one, and even Caleb York didn't relish those odds.

He said to Colman, "But I feel like it now."

"Feel like what?"

Running.

York turned tail and ran back into the cemetery, and as the shots flew, he dove and tumbled and got himself behind a gravestone, a real one, not a wood marker and certainly not a damn cross. He got the .44 out and Colman was yelling, but not at him—at his confederates, telling them to spread out. Probably literal Confederates, considering.

Because his glimpse of the other two had identified these accomplices as part of the Arizona Cowboy crowd, no one he knew by name, but wearers of the telltale rattlesnake hatband, whether genuine article or silversmith copy.

Crouching, York started moving to his right, staying low, the darkness covering him well enough that he didn't draw any fire. As he got close to the south edge of the cemetery, he planted himself behind another sturdy marker and listened.

One of the bastards was moving, too fast, stirring up dust and pebbles enough to be heard.

York popped up, not all the way, just about as high as the stone he was behind, and demonstrated his willingness to shoot a man in the back, or rather in the back of the head, because that was what he did to a Cowboy who was a mere six or seven feet away, close enough for the man's skull to crack and bleed bloody brains like a jam jar burst in a pantry.

Immediately York scrambled toward the west of the cemetery and found cover behind another marker. He huddled there, listening. Whispers and shouts told the story—they were spooked. Spooked in a spooky damn place like this—that was a good one.

He waited.

But after thirty seconds or so had passed, he was afraid they'd be coming around in a pincher move, so he got up and ran. Ran like hell between rows of graves, giving them just enough time to shoot at him and reveal their position, and him enough time to dive for the dirt and let their slugs fly overhead.

One was just behind him, on the same row, and York swivelled onto his back and let fly with three rounds that peppered a Cowboy's midsection and turned him into an awkward floundering thing that seemed to be going in every direction at once, as if chasing the spurts of scarlet in the night that blew out of him like streamers on the Fourth of July.

Scrambling again, on his hands and knees, York got into the next row west and found cover again.

"*York!*"

York didn't respond. The voice was coming from several rows to the east, fairly close to the Cullen mausoleum.

"Caleb York, you son of a bitch! . . . I will holster my weapon if you pledge to holster yours. We will face each other like men!"

York peeked around the gravestone. He could see Colman clearly—the man had his six-gun poised to be stuffed back in his holster.

"All right!" York yelled. "A duel between gentlemen!"

"A duel between goddamn gentlemen! . . . We'll go on the count of three! I'll count, 'less you want to!"

"I trust you, Colman! You do the counting!"

Peeking out, York saw the Cowboy holster his weapon.

York stood and fired three times, each round catching the man in the head, exploding his pretty face and the things behind it into fragments. The dead man, on legs getting no signals, stumbled forward and fell over the nearest gravestone, draped there spilling brains and blood and general gore onto a ground that would not be helped by the irrigation.

"Idiot," York said.

The residents silently agreed.

As he rode under the Circle G archway and past the water tower, barn, and other structures, York saw no sign of the hired gunmen or indeed any of the ranch hands. They must have again either been tending to stock on the range or, most likely, the bulk of them were positioned along the nearby white bank of Sugar Creek, armed to the teeth, ready and waiting.

York tied up at the hitching rail in front of the hacienda-style ranch house and went up the several steps to the porch and found the massive front door unlocked.

He went in.

Byers, the self-described factotum, appeared from somewhere and was immediately flustered. "Mr. York! Sheriff, please! You can't just barge in like—"

York brushed the plump little bookkeeper aside and headed for the door that led to the library/study. He went in and saw, down at the far end of the chamber, Victoria Hammond behind her desk, going over documents. Contracts? Deeds? He didn't really care.

He strode across the lengthy room and leaned over her as she sat there; his hands were flat on the wooden surface of the desktop.

"Where is your son?"

"My . . . my son?"

"Where *is* he, woman?"

She sighed and straightened, gathering her dignity. Lovely, long, dark hair up, she was in a simple white blouse with a few lacy touches and a black bolo tie.

"I won't be spoken to in that manner," she said. "Where is Byers? Why did he admit you without informing me? How dare you—"

"Your son told me you were going to meet me at Boot Hill at dusk. You weren't there. *He* wasn't there."

She flinched. "What are you *talking* about?"

A male voice blurted, "*Stop!*"

York turned and the bookkeeper, a little revolver in a trembling hand, was at the doorway. The small man started to move unsteadily toward York, who walked over calmly, took the gun away from him, slapped him twice, grabbed him by the suit coat, and threw him into the hall, slamming the door on him.

Then the sheriff returned to the desk, where Victoria Hammond was watching this with her mouth hanging open and her dark eyes showing white all around.

"Where were we?" York asked.

"Right here," she said, through her teeth, and her hand came up and revealed her own little revolver, apparently plucked from a nearby drawer.

He reached out and grabbed that gun, too, right out of her hand, startling her. He flung it to the floor hard enough that they were both lucky it didn't go off.

"Now listen, woman," he said, and he told her quietly, calmly, but with rage bubbling, about the meeting her son had arranged.

"Obviously," she said, "I wasn't there."

"Obviously. But Clay Colman was."

She frowned in apparent confusion. "What was my ramrod doing there?"

"Getting killed. By me."

She gasped, and he told her the circumstances, including the other two gun-toting cowhands of hers that he'd also killed.

"So," he said. "Where is your son?"

Seemingly thrown off balance, she said, "He's with the men. He's in charge. . . . Well, he was second-in-command, really, to Clay Colman. But he *thinks* he's in charge."

"You still haven't answered me. Where?"

"With the other men, as I said. Guarding Sugar Creek."

York turned to go.

"*Caleb!* Please. I knew nothing of this. Believe me."

Without looking back at her, but not going anywhere either, he asked, "Why should I?"

He heard her heavy chair screech, being pushed back as she stood.

"Don't go," she said, and came around to him. "Allow me to explain, as best I can."

The door flew open and Byers was there again, a

double-barreled shotgun in hand this time; he looked un-hinged, his hair, his clothes askew.

"Mr. Byers," she said calmly, "the sheriff is my guest. Would you have the girl get us some wine, please? The Casa Madero red."

Byers, his eyes wide, his mouth an O, had to think about that for a moment. Then he swallowed and said, "Yes, mistress."

The factotum, shotgun lowered, closed the door gently behind him.

Victoria Hammond had York by the arm now. She looked up at him, so very beautiful, and said, "Please don't kill Mr. Byers. He'd be terribly difficult to replace."

"Do my best," he said.

York allowed her to lead him to the sitting area over-seen by the looming oil portrait of her dead husband, looking down at them disapprovingly, or at least so it seemed to York. She guided him onto the two-seater sofa and nestled beside him.

"And I don't want you to kill my son Pierce, either," she said, with an enigmatic smile, hands folded in her lap. "You've already taken *one* son from me. Do you want to make me cross?"

He didn't know what to say to that. He didn't even know what to think of it.

"I did not send Clay Colman to kill you," she assured him. "Why would I?"

Because I killed your son? York thought.

"You defended my interests at Sugar Creek," she said. "I appreciate that. You're the law. I *need* the law in this."

York said, "I know why Colman wanted me dead."

Interested, as if he had suggested a book she might care to read, she said, "Really? Why?"

"I killed two friends of his. Stagecoach bandits. Years ago. He was one, too, but got away from me."

"Why didn't you bring him in, when you saw him working here for me? Isn't that what you do? Arrest them or . . . shoot them?"

"He was just a suspect in that robbery," York said. "I hardly ever shoot suspects."

"You do have your standards."

"Is that what you intend to do? Rib me?"

The serving girl came in with a tray of glasses and a carafe of red wine. Poured for them both and York thanked her, while the mistress of the Circle G did not. The girl went out.

"No," Victoria Hammond said. "It's just that . . . some things are just so terribly sad that sometimes a person simply has to laugh or go mad. Don't you find that to be the case?"

"Not particularly. Why would your son help Colman set me up if he wasn't doing your bidding?"

Now she did seem closer to tears than laughter.

She sipped her wine. Said, "He's a young, impetuous boy. He loved his brother, so he would obviously resent you for taking William away from him . . . *and* he wants to impress me. Wants to show his mother that he's a man, capable of . . ."

"Murder?"

"No. He wasn't there, at the cemetery, was he? No, he's fallen under Clay Colman's spell, I'm afraid. Ever since I assigned him to ride at Colman's side, he's tried to be one of them, those men. Strong like them."

"Well, nobody's under Colman's spell now." York had some wine. Not bad. "Victoria, you have to put a stop to this. If your men take part in this water-rights war, I will start arresting them."

She frowned in frustration. "But we're in the right."

"No. It's clear you have assembled a band of cut-throats to do your dirty work. You *want* a war. You lied to me, or led me astray anyway, by indicating you planned to make a good offer to Willa Cullen for the Bar-O. Then you offered her peanuts. You didn't even salt the damn things."

"It was . . . a tactic."

He looked at her, stern. "Let this play out legally. This is your land. You'll likely come out on top. If you don't, and you recklessly kill your neighbor's cowhands, and cause her stock to die of thirst, you may face legal and certainly civil ramifications."

Her expression now was thoughtful. "What would you suggest?"

"Just take a step back. Turn down the heat. You should limit this to a couple of campsites on the Sugar Creek banks, keeping watch. If the Bar-O roars back with a passel of men, you have a right to defend yourself."

"You're suggesting that if I make an effort to curtail the violence, it will look better. In court. And to the Trinidad citizens."

He shook his head. "I'm suggesting you do it because it's the right thing. If you don't, I might have to raise a posse and wade in and stop people on each side. Fill my jail with both your crew and Willa's."

"The ones you don't kill."

"I've never killed a man who didn't pull on me first."

"Not that you'll admit to."

They were looking right at each other, close enough to touch noses.

"Not that I admit to, no," he said. "Can you give me

one good reason not to haul your son in for aiding and abetting attempted murder? *My* attempted murder?"

She kissed him.

It was warm and slow and seemed to tell him things. No, *did* tell him things. He hadn't pulled away, at first as startled as if she'd slapped him, but then he just got caught up in it, in the sensuousness of it, the lilac scent of her.

She moved herself up to where she was sitting in his lap and kissed him again and, without any sense that he'd willed it, his arms went around her and he held her to him and the kiss went on and on. . . .

Finally it ended, but her face was still near his when she said, "I've wanted you since the moment I saw you, Caleb. I knew of you, I'd heard of you, but it seemed . . . it had to be an exaggeration. Men like you just don't exist. Men so strong." She moved her bottom as if trying to find a more comfortable place in his lap.

Not that *he* was comfortable.

Then he got hold of himself, and of her, and lifted her by her narrow waist above the sweep of her hips and set her down gently but firmly beside him on the love seat.

He said, "I need you to reduce your men's presence on Sugar Creek."

She nodded, breathing hard. "Two campsites. Two men per campsite. I promise."

"Good. Good." He stood.

Her husband glowered down.

She rose, took his arm, led him slowly to the door, as if sending her man off to serve in a war somewhere. And wasn't she?

"When this is over," she said, "I will need someone strong by my side at this place."

He told her what he'd told Willa so many times: "I'm no cattleman."

"I don't want a man to head up a cattle drive or fix a fence and rope a calf. I want a man with sand who can stand up to challenges. A man smart enough to make hard decisions, who understands that business is a perilous but oh so profitable affair. I can offer you so much, Caleb . . . so much."

She deposited him in the hallway and shut the door softly on him, sealing herself in the library. Byers was nowhere to be seen. York found his way to the door.

As he stood near the gelding, like a man who'd fallen down a flight of stairs but didn't seem to be damaged in particular, he nonetheless felt shaken.

And suspicious.

But all the way out to the main road, he wondered.

Wondered what a night with that woman would be like.

CHAPTER THIRTEEN

With a full moon and a starry sky lighting the way, Caleb York, on his way back to Trinidad, paused at the mouth of the Circle G lane at the irregular excuse for a main road, where telegraph poles, post-blizzard, still tilted at awkward angles. The pole closest pointed in the opposite direction of town—to the fairly nearby artery to the Bar-O.

York sucked in breath, let it out as a sigh, and guided the gelding north.

Awkward though it surely would be, talking to Willa was a duty that best not be shirked. On the way, he imagined what he'd say to her and got nowhere, encouraging his horse to just lope along. As he rode at an easy trot into the Bar-O grounds with its corral, grain crib, water tower, cook's shack, bunkhouse, and ranch house—the only signs of life were the yellow glow of lamplight in a few windows of the latter two.

So York didn't see her at first, sitting in the dark on the porch in a chair her father had fashioned. Not till his horse was hitched and he'd gone up the steps and was standing with fist poised to pound on the door.

"I'm here," Willa said quietly.

She was in denims and a green-and-black plaid shirt and her bare feet. Usually, with her yellow hair braided up, she brought to mind a young Viking woman, waiting for her warrior husband's return from his plunder. Tonight she looked small. Like a girl. Waiting for nobody at all.

He walked over to her, footsteps echoing on the wooden planking, spurs singing a melancholy tune. Positioning himself before her, he took the liberty of leaning back against the porch railing. He took his hat off, brushed back his hair. A lamp in the window behind her put half of her in darkness.

The half of her in light was enough to let him see the handgun in her lap—a .22 Colt Open Top Model revolver, pearl handled, with fancy engraving. Her father had given it to her for her eighteenth birthday, York knew. Capable of seven deadly shots.

He said, "I've spoken to Victoria Hammond again."

"Have you." Her voice was soft, uninflected, her blue eyes fixed on him, rarely blinking.

"She's agreed to pull her men off the banks of the creek," he said, nodding in that direction. "Just a handful are keeping watch now at two campfires."

Her voice still soft, she said, "More than a dozen men were on the shore and above, on the grassy patch by the pines, this afternoon."

He held up a palm. "I just came from the Circle G. She's agreed not to let this thing get any further out of hand."

"Has she."

The front door opened and someone stepped out. For

a moment York didn't know who it was, but then he realized it was her foreman, Bill Jackson. He wore no hat,
but was in a gray sparkly sateen shirt and brown duck
trousers, wearing no sidearm. Looked like he'd been
making himself at home.

At least he wasn't barefoot, too.

Jackson frowned—not threateningly, but a frown.
"What's this about?"

What was he *now? The man of the damn house?*

Half turning, York said to him, "I've convinced the
Hammond woman to back off at Sugar Creek."

Jackson spoke as he came over to plant himself with
York to his left and the seated Willa to his right.

"How did you manage that?" he asked the sheriff.

Patiently, York said, "I told her what I'm about to tell
the two of you. That I am prepared to put a posse together to shut down both sides in this squabble. To
charge anybody who starts shooting, and anybody who
shoots back, with assault or worse. And throw their tails
in jail."

Jackson's laugh was curt. "You're the only one here
who's fired a shot so far."

"I know, and I'll shoot again, if I have to." He sent his
eyes to Willa, whose oval face, glowing in the near dark,
was as unmoving as a carved ivory cameo. "You and the
Hammond woman need to let your lawyers work this
thing out."

Jackson grunted a nonlaugh. "And in the meantime let
our cattle die of thirst?"

"Our" cattle?

"Those steers'll die all the sooner," York said tightly,
"if they're stampeded in the middle of a gun battle. Or if
it's just men fighting it out, this time it won't be dead

cows floating and fouling the water." He looked at her, hard. "You two women need to stop feuding and turn your lawyers loose . . . and tell them to negotiate fast and fair."

Her eyes tightened, but her voice remained neutral. "You'd have me sell to that witch?"

He gave his head a single shake. "That's not my concern in this."

"It isn't?"

"No. Keeping the peace is."

Jackson gestured to the .44 at York's right hip. "And that's the peacekeeper you use to do that with, correct?"

York shrugged. "Sometimes that's what it takes."

The foreman lurched forward and got his face right in York's. "How much is Victoria Hammond paying you, exactly, Sheriff?"

"Not a red cent."

Jackson's breath was hot on York's face. "Maybe it isn't with money. Maybe it's something else."

York shoved him, and Jackson came back with a roundhouse swing that the sheriff ducked, coming up with a solid right fist that rocked the foreman, lifting the man's chin and staggering him back. The two were poised with fists clenched, ready to make much more of it when Willa said, firm, not a scream, "Stop, you two!"

They stopped.

York felt embarrassed, and it was clear so did Jackson.

"Bill," she said, on her feet now, "go inside. Please."

The foreman looked at her, then at York, and back at her. "Are you . . . sure?"

She nodded. "I'm quite sure." She pointed to the door. "Go."

Clearly not liking being treated like a child, Jackson

sighed, glowered at York, then shuffled over and went inside, having at least enough dignity left not to slam the door.

York and Willa were standing on the porch now, facing each other.

Nodding toward the ranch house, York said, "So, Jackson *lives* here now?"

She frowned, disgusted. "He's in the guest room. He insisted."

"Oh, he did, did he?"

"He felt I might be in danger. He said he wanted to post a man in the house with a gun to protect me."

"He wasn't wearing one. Anyway, *you* have a gun."

"I do," she said, lifting the little weapon in her palm. "And Victoria Hammond has a whole lot of guns."

He felt silly, all of a sudden. And a hypocrite—what right did he have being jealous of that black cowboy, after sitting in a love seat with Victoria Hammond?

"Listen," York said, holding his hands up in surrender, doing his best to sound reasonable, "just try to keep this from exploding for a few days. Raymond Parker is working behind the scenes on this mess, and—"

She frowned. "*Parker?* How? What does he have in mind?"

"He didn't share everything with me." And most of what Parker *had* shared with Caleb, the businessman wanted the sheriff to keep to himself.

"For now," York told her, and almost settled a hand on her shoulder, "tell your man Jackson to send some scouts ahead, through the brush and trees on the east side of the creek. They need to keep out of sight, but confirm that the Hammond woman has withdrawn her men."

"And if she hasn't?"

"Send a rider to town and let me know, at once. I'll get right on putting a posse together."

Her expression was damn near mocking. "Of Trinidad town folk?"

He waved that off. "No. I'll do what you and Victoria Hammond did—go to Las Vegas and come back with some dangerous dregs."

"Funny way of keeping the peace."

"It's not a solution I'm partial to, but it's what I've got."

Her eyes tightened again, yet her expression softened, and her voice had hurt in it when she asked, "Caleb . . . *why?*"

"Why what?"

Now anger came out. "Why did you side *against* me in this?"

He sucked in air and let it right back out. "Damn it, woman! You talked me into keeping this job and the badge that came with it. Hell, I have *two* of the damn things now! If I had scurried to your feet like a lap dog, would you have liked it? Loved me for it? Or would you have lost all respect for me?"

She had no answer.

"I'll say good night then," he said, and tugged on his hat. He began to go, but paused and said, "Will you promise me one thing?"

"What's that?"

"You'll let the men do the fighting."

She smiled. "Would you love me for it? Or would you lose all respect for me?"

Now he had no answer.

But he went back to her, and kissed her pretty mouth, gently, and so quick she couldn't return it or refuse it.

Not much of a kiss, in the scheme of things, but as he

rode back to Trinidad it occurred to him how much more it meant than that show of passion another woman had forced on him.

Victoria Hammond supervised in her kitchen, but she was not cooking up a feast, at least not literally.

After all, she wasn't even wearing an apron. Instead, the dark-eyed beauty was in black, if no longer in mourning; rather, she was decked out in a black leather vest over a black shirt above black gaucho-style pants. High on her right hip rode a Colt Single Action .45 with mother-of-pearl grips boasting an eagle and snake pattern; her heavy Mexican-style leather holster was beautifully tooled and stamped with a floral design.

Few hostesses in the Southwest were more distinctively turned out.

Feast or not, something in this kitchen was cooking, all right, and she did have a chef of sorts, who was sitting midpoint at the eight-foot rustic Mexican table, as were several interested students. Three soup bowls and a larger serving bowl were set out in a horizontal row in front of him. One soup bowl contained a serving of black powder, another shimmered with viscous glue, and the third collected some shreds of tree bark. The larger bowl was empty.

The chef—more like a chief, in his faded blue army jacket, red silk bandanna, and with that ebony hair, parted in the middle, braids to his shoulders—was handsome enough to stir things in Victoria. Those ice-blue eyes, the high cheekbones, and that square jaw—he was a living bronze statue created by a master sculptor. Yet they called this man a kid.

The Chiricahua Kid.

Seated at the table with the Apache were the other two dangerous men the late Clay Colman had hired in Las Vegas: Dave Carson, boyish and skimpily mustached with close-set eyes, making him look dumber than he was; and Billy Bassett, lean and heavily mustached, older than any of the rest of her crop of riders.

"You're the leader now, Mr. Bassett," she had told him, after she learned of Colman's fate at the hands of Caleb York.

"In my mind," Bassett admitted, "I always was."

They'd been talking in the library, Victoria behind the desk, the gunhand before her like a soldier reporting to a general.

She asked, "You scouted the position?"

Bassett nodded. "There's a rise behind the bunkhouse and barn. Not much of one, but enough. Job can be done from there."

"You took the Indian with you?"

"I did."

"His appraisal?"

A shrug. "Said it looked okay."

"Elaborate praise, coming from him."

"Don't say much, it's true."

The other person at the kitchen table, watching the Kid prepare for what was to come, was her middle son, Pierce. He was wearing an outfit he'd bought back home in Colorado, to prepare for the Circle G and what he saw as his new role as a genuine man of the West—a buckskin jacket with fringed sleeves and matching buckskin trousers and buckskin moccasins.

She did not know whether to laugh or cry.

But at least he was trying. He'd done well for her, arranging at her request the meeting—ambush, really—

with Colman at the cemetery; it was Colman who'd fumbled that.

Tonight would be a chance for Pierce to learn about himself. And for Victoria to learn about him, for better or worse.

Bassett, an interested pupil, said, "This the way you savages burned out settlers?"

"Some time," the Indian affirmed. "Mainly for making signal at night."

The Kid poured the bowl of gloppy glue into the bigger bowl, then dumped in the gunpowder, like he was overpeppering a stew. With his right hand, he stirred the mixture briefly, then rubbed the residue on his fingers off on a rag. Finally, from a pile of arrows next to the bowl, he plucked the head off one and dragged the wooden shaft through the black powder, tipping the bowl to do so. He never spilled a drop.

The gunpowder was soon coating the wood, as thick as a quarter of an inch around, save for a few bare inches at the bottom of the shaft, which he held on to. With his free hand, the Kid took a strip of bark from the remaining bowl and bit off a bite, as if it were beef jerky. He chewed. He chewed some more. Then he removed the wad of masticated bark from his mouth and dipped it in the remaining gunpowder. He fastened the result to the tip of the stick.

Transfixed, Pierce said, "So then you set that nubbin on fire?"

The Kid nodded.

"How?" Pierce wondered.

"How," the Indian said, puzzled.

"I mean, do you, uh, rub some sticks together and—"

"No. Kitchen match."

The Kid repeated the process, making himself half a dozen such arrows. He handed one each to the men at the table to hold by the shaft's uncoated end and allow the result to dry for a while. Soon Bassett and Carson and Victoria's son were each holding an arrow in a fist. The Kid was holding up one himself. It looked a little absurd, Victoria had to admit. Like some secret ceremony, or like diners waiting for food to be served and then speared.

Eyes narrowed as he glanced around the table, Bassett asked, "Six? That's all? Don't you want a few more?"

The Kid seemed to be thinking about blinking, but didn't. "Why?"

"In case you miss."

"Billy, what a lucky man."

"Who, me?"

The Kid nodded. "You. Kid don't kill friends."

Victoria laughed. But was he kidding? Either way, she liked the Apache. With Colman gone, she was getting ideas that went beyond the festivities planned for the evening.

The Kid turned to Pierce. "Could use your help."

Pierce's eyes were big. "Me? Help from *me*?"

The Kid nodded.

"Right *now*?"

"No. On hilltop."

"Oh. Okay."

"I put arrow on bowstring. Aim. Then lower bow with arrow not shot yet, and you light up tip. I raise bow and let fly. Shoot high. Give time for flame to grow. Arrow comes down and hits where I aim . . . and then, time for another arrow."

Pierce smiled like Christmas morning. "You trust me with this, Kid?"

"If your mama do, I do."

His eyes sought her approval. "Do you, Mother?"

She took one of the drying arrows from him and pressed the box of kitchen matches in his hand by way of reply.

CHAPTER FOURTEEN

When her foreman got back, Willa Cullen was still sitting on the porch, taking in the quiet of a moon-swept, star-flung night, enjoying the caress of a cool breeze from the south. Shortly after Caleb had ridden off, she had summoned Jackson to take Frank Duffy and Buck O'Fallon, the two remaining shootists from the Las Vegas hiring, to get a clandestine look at the Sugar Creek shoreline.

Now Jackson stood next to his seated employer, hat in hand, and reported.

"York was truth tellin'," Jackson said, looking like he wished what he was saying weren't gospel. "There's two campsites, two Circle G men at each one. Well spread apart. Could be others are posted in the pines, but we couldn't spot 'em. And with the moon makin' noon out of the night, I think we likely would."

She nodded, agreeing with that assessment. "You left Duffy and O'Fallon behind, I take it?"

"Positioned in those woods, each with a view on a campsite. Any activity, they'll report back."

"Good."

Neither said anything for a while.

Then Willa looked up at him and asked, "Can we afford to give this a few days, d'you think?"

He drew a breath, exhaled, then shrugged. "Water tower's damn near dry. They's a water hole to the north that may let us stretch things out a bit. This fellow Parker that York talks about—is he an ally?"

She nodded again. "He's a good man. He and my papa and another man built the Bar-O. If anybody can find a way around this . . . a way *out* of it . . . it's Raymond L. Parker."

Jackson's half smile was sour. "Well, *York* only knows one thing—that .44 on his hip."

She knew that wasn't true, but said nothing.

"I can't believe I'm saying this," she said wryly, "but maybe we should take that Hammond woman at her word."

They mulled it a while, and then—as if evidence were being presented in the matter—a burst of flame flared out of the darkness, above the bunkhouse, like low-hanging Fourth of July fireworks. She didn't see it, but Jackson did.

"What the hell . . ." he began.

She turned toward where he was looking. The second burst of flame she saw all right, and then the oversized shack that was the bunkhouse took another hit from what was now apparently a flame-tipped arrow.

In seconds the building's flat roof was ablaze.

She got to her feet, but Jackson was already on the run, slamming on his hat, heading off the porch and down the steps, and charging across the open hard-dirt apron, his .38 Colt Lightning revolver in hand.

Her first thought was: *Does he think he can fight fire with bullets?* But her second thought was more apt: *We're under attack!*

Here at the far end of the porch, facing the bunkhouse—enough distance between it and the ranch house to make the fire spreading here not an immediate danger—she positioned herself with the .22 Colt handgun her father had given her, years ago.

Apparently more arrows had struck the back of the bunkhouse, because fiery fingers were reaching around both sides of the wooden structure, as if to take it in a terrible searing grip. Jackson was at the door of the shack, struggling to remove a thick branch that had been jammed in through the door handle to block entry . . . or, more importantly, exit.

Someone had managed to sneak around and insert that thing without her seeing it, even as she'd been sitting right here on this porch! It would have taken someone incredibly deft, capable of the sneaking silence of . . .

. . . an Indian. The kind of Indian who could send fiery arrows into the night, and turn a bunkhouse into a charnel house.

Jackson had reported seeing an Indian among the Circle G men at Sugar Creek, and Buck O'Fallon thought it had been the Chiricahua Kid, a notorious renegade Apache turned outlaw.

Could this be his handiwork?

These thoughts raced through her mind, as she watched her foreman working to get that branch loose and out, which he did, casting it aside; but the flames were encroaching his position, the entire building swarming with dancing demons of orange and yellow and blue. Men within were shouting. Screaming. . . .

And by the time he got the door open, the men who came running out through billowing smoke were already burning, glowing, shrieking, probably rushing from the back of the building, where arrows had apparently hit the rear exterior walls, the other men within getting out of the way of the flaming figures, comrades they couldn't help and hoped to avoid.

The race the burning men were running didn't last long—they made only a few yards before flopping to the ground and soon the only movement coming from the crisply blackened figures were the flames emanating like a ghastly victory dance. The other men came stumbling out, coughing, hands over their faces. The bunkhouse was lost under the blanket of flickering orange-blue, the roar of the conflagration punctuated by crackling, a din so ear-filling that it took a few moments for the hoofbeats to register . . .

. . . *hoofbeats of horses carrying a dozen-plus men, an invading army coming down the lane and charging into the open hard-dirt apron around which the outbuildings and ranch house were arranged. Handguns blazed their own little jagged orange fires as rounds were triggered into the staggering cowboys who didn't even have time to know how they were dying or at whose hands.*

From her perch on the porch, Willa began returning fire and two men tumbled from the saddles, plummeting to the ground, dead or dying, their horses charging on without them. The onslaught was something of a blur, but she recognized certain riders as being of the Arizona rustling bunch, the so-called Cowboys, who'd recently been hired on at the Circle G.

In between the burning bunkhouse and the oncoming riders, on the slight slope where the only thing alive about the charred dead men sprawled on the grass was the flames dancing on their backs, knelt Bill Jackson, cool and steady and still as he carefully picked off intruders, one, two, three. . . .

But from behind the inferno that had been the bunkhouse scurried an absurd figure in fringed buckskin, a young man on foot, boyish but not a boy—*wasn't that one of Victoria Hammond's sons?* Like a refugee from a Wild West show, the buckskin cowboy, gun in hand, drew a bead on the kneeling Jackson, who did not see this ridiculous threat coming.

She screamed a warning, but the whoops and war cries of the invading force—whittled by a third now—merged with the growl of the vortex of flame and drowned her out. The crack of the gunshot got lost in the general clamor, but she saw the spurt of blood, a ribbon of red unfurling, exiting Jackson's left temple, and he tottered for just a moment, already dead before falling onto his side, like a milk bottle hit by a County Fair ball.

Young Hammond had an awful smile on his face, an odd combination of glee and horror. But he didn't wear it long. Willa took aim with that .22 in her fist, just as she had when her father taught her to shoot tin cans for practice. She fired twice and both rounds hit the buckskin figure in the chest, and he took the bullets like he'd been shoved there, twice. Not hard. Just shoved.

He looked down at himself, at two black holes that wept single scarlet tears, then gazed across the open area at Willa standing there with gunsmoke twirling like a tiny lariat from her gun barrel. The glee left, the horror remained, and then he took two tentative steps, with the gun still in hand, before falling flat on his boyish face.

Wielding a double-barreled shotgun, plump, whitebearded Harmon emerged from his cookhouse, in a red long john top and britches he'd thrown on—he slept in back—and let one barrel's worth blow a rider off his saddle. Then he repeated the activity and reloaded.

Over by the horse barn—the burning bunkhouse sending sparks and cinders treacherously its way—lanky old Lou Morgan, the wrangler in charge there, was kneeling with his Winchester taking aim and bringing down more riders, calm as a hunter sighting a deer. And another deer. And another.

Though they were outnumbered heavily—just Willa and the cookie and wrangler and the now dead foreman—the invaders were getting driven back. Or maybe it was just that the attackers had accomplished what they'd set out to, now that every one of the cowhands who'd been in that bunkhouse been sent to heaven or hell, as the case might be.

At any rate, the raiders were gone as quick as they'd come, leaving a stirring of dust by way of farewell.

Willa stood and breathed hard, through the acrid taste and smell of smoke. She assessed the situation, sending her eyes around her property. The shack where those men had once slept before fiery death came knocking was spitting embers and cinders at the nearby barn. It would be only a matter of time before that building caught fire, too—the wind blowing north was the only saving grace thus far—and, of course, that was the structure within which all their horses were stabled.

No more contemplation.

Time to get to work.

She gathered Harmon and they joined Morgan, whom she told, "We need to start leading the horses from the barn into the corral."

Morgan said gruffly, "Much as I prefer equines, should we first check the fallen?"

"No," she said. "Our people are dead. Incinerated or shot or both."

"What if some of theirs is breathing?"

"They can wait their turn. Our horses come first."

The old boy had no argument with that.

But he did say, "I best at least gather their weapons."

She nodded. "Do that. Pile them over by the house."

The wrangler started in on that, and Willa and Harmon moved quickly into the barn, where the horses were stirring, their neighs and whinnies as hysterical as their wild-eyed faces. They calmed the animals as best they could, and she and the cook swiftly began a one-at-a-time exodus. Morgan joined in a few minutes later, and the barn indeed did start to burn, but the last animal was conveyed out of there before the whole place and all the hay in it went up with a bellow like a wounded beast behind them. The bigger size of the structure, easily three times what the bunkhouse had been, illuminated the world of carnage around them—black corpses, bloodied corpses—making a terrible day out of what had begun a gentle night.

For one endless moment, the three survivors stood there facing the burning barn with their pale flesh echoing by way of flickery reflections the blaze before them.

"More to do," she told the two men.

Next the mistress of the ranch and her two remaining hands gathered the milling horses from which the dead invaders had fallen. Some of the raiders' animals had run off into the dark, but the rest—half a dozen—the trio rounded up and put in the corral, saddles and all.

Over by the house, Morgan's pile of weapons—handguns and rifles—was an impressive reminder of the extent of the onslaught. That the three of them had survived it seemed a small miracle. Maybe not so small. But the truth was even Harmon had held his own and both Willa and Morgan were damn good shots.

And men on horseback, however used to battle or gunplay a steed might be, were subject to controlling the animal conveying them, and had reins to deal with as well as weapons. No easy task.

Willa gathered her troops—both of them, the fat cook and the old cowboy.

"Let's haul their dead over there," she said, pointing to where black human timbers lay smoking, some still sizzling. "We'll want to keep the area around the corral clear."

Harmon looked a little queasy at the suggestion, which of course was not a suggestion at all, but an order. Morgan didn't mind. He'd fought Rebs and Indians in his day. So they went around taking the dead men by the wrists and dragging them like bags of seed that fell off a wagon.

Willa paused in her work only twice. First, to look with a certain sadness at the boy in buckskin. No, not a boy—probably going on thirty, but pale and soft and with hands that had never seen a day of real work. She could hardly have hated Victoria Hammond more, yet she still felt a brief pang of pity for the woman, losing a second son in a few days, and again to violence.

But just a pang. And brief.

As for taking this young man's life, Willa felt nothing much—certainly not guilt, only a sadness that the Hammond offspring had been subjected to an upbringing by such a monstrous mother, who had set him on a path that had led him here, to lie dead on the ground among the charred remains and bullet-ridden bodies of others who had died in service of a woman seeking wealth and power.

The second time she paused was to kneel next to the dead Bill Jackson and pray for his soul. Before she stood, she kissed his forehead. This man shot and killed, that was a loss. You could rebuild a barn or a bunkhouse, but a dead man was gone forever.

She was surprised to discover that, among the fallen, no Indian lay. Nor had she seen one among the fleeing raiders. Not the Chiricahua Kid nor any other. She'd felt certain those flaming arrows were the work of that hostile brave, corrupted by white men. Unless some veteran of the Indian wars had picked up the skill needed to craft and dispatch those fiery missiles. But she doubted it.

Again, the hoarse howl of flames, interspersed with snaps and an insistent crackling, muted the sound of others approaching. Morgan noticed it first and came over and pointed out the buckboard coming down the lane, two men in the seat. They seemed in no hurry.

"Recognize them?" she asked the old wrangler.

"Can't say I do. Must be somebody saw the fire and smoke in the sky, and come to see if we need help."

The driver slowed and both men offered mild smiles and nodded at Willa and Morgan, who were out in the midst of the hard-dirt area between burning buildings and the ranch house and corral. The driver had a mustache that overwhelmed his face and looked to be forty at least, while the rider was a good ten years younger, also mustached but not so full, kind of dumb looking, with close-set eyes hugging his nose.

"My lord," the driver said, frowning around at the grisly scene, "this here is more than just a damn fire. What happened, anyways?"

Willa said, "Raiders from a rival ranch hit us."

"Hell you say. You need any help?"

"No, we'll be riding into town for that."

The rider said, "Maybe we could help carry buckets over from the water tower, and try to put out that blaze 'fore it claims any other buildings."

"Not enough water in that tower," she said, "to give my flower garden a drink. No, but we appreciate your offer."

"Okay, then," the driver said. "I'll just turn this buggy around."

The heavily mustached driver guided the two horses hauling the four-wheeled wagon into a half circle, but then paused. A tarp covering something in the back—no, not something, *someone*—got flipped aside and a figure rose to what seemed a towering height . . . a woman in black with blazing black eyes and a wild mane of ebony hair and a .45 in a gloved fist.

Victoria Hammond shot Willa and the bullet tore through Willa's upper chest at her right shoulder like a searing hot lance had gone through her. She fell to her knees as the Hammond woman fired again, but missed, only Willa dropped onto her left side, perhaps giving the shooter the sense that the second bullet *had* hit.

Harmon had set his shotgun against the corral fence and he was scrambling for it when Victoria shot him in the back of the head. Morgan had leaned his Winchester against the side of the house, and he ran for it, but Victoria picked him off like a bird on the fly, grinning as she did.

Willa saw this, although later she wondered if she only *thought* she saw it, that maybe she had conjured a memory of the shootings from what she'd heard, and only imagined seeing such a beautiful face twisted into so ugly an evil mask.

After that, she really did only hear things.

Victoria saying, "Gather him."

In a strangely gentle voice.

The two men climbing down from the buckboard.

"Put him in back with me," she said. "Gentle. Gentle."

Oh, Willa thought. *She's collecting her son.*

That must have distracted the grieving mother, kept her from doing what Willa knew the woman should have done, which was put a bullet in her fallen rival's head.

But then the buckboard rattled off, again in no hurry, and the noisy hell of the burning barn was the only thing that kept Willa approaching a state of wakefulness.

Still, it took time for her to even *think* about getting up, though she was never sure how long she lay there. Numbness had set right in, around the wound, fore and aft. The bullet seemed to have gone straight through her, not hitting any bone, not careening around, tearing things up in her. Then the burning sensation started, and it may have helped keep her from passing out.

Finally she managed to get to her feet, as if reassembling herself from scattered parts, and stumbled over to the corral, and through the gate, where she took the first saddled horse she came to and somehow, somehow, got herself up and on.

She eased the horse out of the corral. Stopped and looked at her fallen comrades—skinny old Morgan, no man better with a horse . . . plump old Harmon, best cookie any ranch ever knew. She swallowed hard, with no sense of the tears streaking down her soot-covered face.

Then she rode back to town. At a steady pace, holding on to the reins, working every second of the way to keep her balance and stay awake and not fall off and die on the road before she could get to town.

To town and Caleb York.

CHAPTER FIFTEEN

For a Saturday night, business was slow at the Victory Saloon, with no sign of the usual payday bustle. Satin-and-silk gals just sitting around, piano player entertaining himself. Chuck-a-luck and roulette with nary a taker. Only a few dusty cowhands slaking their thirst, outnumbered for once by Hub Wainwright and his quartet of white-shirt, bow-tie bartenders behind the interminable, superbly polished oak bar. Seemed all the Bar-O and Circle G hands were otherwise occupied tonight.

Caleb York, both his badges tucked away in his black frock coat's breast pocket, was having a hair of the dog— but just a hair—as he sat at the round, green-felt-topped table with four City Council members. He had, since strolling in an hour ago, been systematically taking back the money he'd lately lost to them.

And he didn't even seem to be thinking about his cards, just playing automatically if with his usual skill. This annoyed and frustrated the council members, who tried to strike back by playing more aggressively . . . and right into his (poker) hands.

In fact, York really wasn't thinking about his cards. Coming back to town, he'd caught up with Tulley, who was about to start his night rounds, and told the deputy that trouble was coming. That tomorrow morning the sheriff would be riding to Las Vegas, to hire on a posse of hard cases, and Tulley would be on his own for much of the day. No time for napping.

"Cut back on your rounds tonight," York had advised him, "if need be."

"It's come to shootin'?" Tully had asked.

"It will soon enough."

York was mulling what strategy he'd use with the posse of hired guns who'd be riding with him—return to the east bank of the creek? Perhaps divide into two groups and ride into the ranch house grounds even as the other group took the shore? No, that would create a crossfire.

As he absently hauled in chips, and the mayor and other merchants traded discouraged expressions, he explored his options. He won another pot as two men burst through the batwings and into the Victory, took off their hats, and strode over to position themselves beside him, in a supplicating manner. They looked glum. Both had blood on their shirts.

York recognized them as Willa's men, two of the Vegas gunfighters she'd brought on: Frank Duffy and Buck O'Fallon. Their reputations, while not spotless, were certainly more nearly shining than the ruthless man-killers hired by Victoria Hammond.

Tall, broad shouldered, black haired, with a tanned, weathered look about him, Duffy said, "Sheriff, you best come with us. Miss Cullen has been shot."

York was on his feet at once, and the City Council members looked stunned, alarmed, as well they should. He said, "Not . . . ?"

"Not killed, but bad wounded."

Former lawman O'Fallon, smallish, with an educated manner, slim where his companion was sinewy, hung on to his broad-brimmed hat with both hands. "Flaming arrows, probably the Chiricahua Kid's doing, set the bunkhouse afire. Then the Hammond crew rode in and started shooting everybody as they came out."

Duffy said, "There was complete mayhem ensued. Every hand shot and killed. Barn burned down. House is standing—that's about all's left."

"Where is Willa now?"

"Doc Miller's. Your deputy helped us take her there."

York practically ran out of the Victory, slamming on his hat, brushing past Rita, who'd overheard all of it, aghast. He got more details on the way.

Seemed the two gunhands had been surreptitiously stationed in the scrubby woods near Sugar Creek, keeping an eye on the shoreline and the men keeping guard at two small campfires there. Then, in the direction of the Bar-O, they saw smoke rising into the night against a blush of orange-yellow that was something other than dawn coming way early.

They had left their post and gone back to the main road and ridden toward the ranch only to encounter a nearly unconscious Willa Cullen, riding toward town, wounded, struggling not to fall off her horse.

Light glowed in the windows of Miller's surgery on the second floor of the bank building. With the two Bar-O hirelings trailing him, York went quickly up the exterior steps hugging the side brick wall to the little landing and went into the waiting room.

Tulley was pacing like an expectant father. He stopped in place when York and the two others burst in.

"That witch shot her, Caleb York! Shot that sweet gal!" The deputy pointed to the place on himself.

"Is she conscious?"

It was Miller who answered, coming out of the surgery: "She's in and out."

The doctor was in the rolled-up sleeves of a bloody shirt, rubbing his hands with an alcohol-soaked cloth.

York faced him. "She going to pull through?"

Miller's shrug made no commitment. "Too early. She's lost blood. I can give her a saline solution as a blood substitute—that can be effective at times."

"At times?"

Another shrug. "Best option I have. It's more successful than the goat milk transfusions we used to give. She's a tough little gal." He bobbed his head back toward his small adjacent surgery. "She heard your voice out here. Wants to speak to you, Caleb. I've given her a sedative that will kick in soon, so you should go in now."

He did.

She lay on her back on the mahogany examination table looking pretty despite the circumstances, but pale as death. The table was heavy, good size, covered in crisp white paper. Her green-and-black shirt had been flung to the floor, her camisole cut away to allow application of a bandage, the gauze stained red.

Her blue eyes were half-lidded, but she smiled, seeing him, when he leaned in over her, taking her near hand.

"Caleb," she said. "Caleb . . ."

He summoned a reassuring smile. "The doc will take good care of you. You just rest."

Her eyes managed to open a little wider. "That woman . . . she and two of her . . . crew. Came in after . . . after her raiders had gone. Must've cut their number in half. *She* did this, Caleb. Shot me."

He gently squeezed the hand. "You just rest. I'll take care of it. Doc'll take care of you."

The eyes were even wider now. "Caleb . . . watch out for her. She's . . . crazed."

"I'll watch out. You rest."

"I set her off!"

"Quiet now . . . I'm going. . . ."

"I killed her boy."

"What?"

She swallowed. "Pierce Hammond . . . he killed Jackson. Bill Jackson. And I shot him for it."

And Victoria had shot Willa for that.

Some women wanted sweet talk, especially at a time like this.

But York told her what he knew she'd want to hear: "I'll make her pay. I'll make them all pay."

Back in the jailhouse office, York conferred with the two Bar-O gunmen and his deputy. The sheriff sat behind his desk, methodically filling every empty loop on his cartridge belt with a .44 bullet. When he was finished, he stood and slung the gun belt on. Buckled it.

"If I were in a mood to wait till morning," York said, "I could ride to Las Vegas and gather a posse with this."

He reached in his inside frock coat pocket and withdrew the lump of brownbacks. He tossed the fold of cash onto the desk, where it made a satisfying thump. The two hired guns looked at the wad of money the way starving men look at their first meal in a long time. Tulley, on the other hand, regarded it like a pile of paper.

"Or," York said, flipping a hand, "we could handle this tonight. Two-way split."

Tulley had done the ciphering. "They is four of us, Caleb York."

"This is not a matter of money to me," York said to

them all. Then to Tulley: "Anyway, Deputy, you and I are already being paid by the county."

"That be a fact," Tulley admitted.

Duffy was still staring at the loot, but O'Fallon's gaze had settled on York. "Handle it tonight *how*?"

"Take them on," the sheriff said calmly. "Right now. When they least expect it."

O'Fallon's eyes were narrow in thought. "How many of the Circle G bunch are left?"

York shook his head. "No idea. But they took heavy losses, Willa said."

"Said the same to us," Duffy said, finally looking up from the cash. "Where you figure they'll be?"

York said, "Could be in their own bunkhouse."

"Oughta burn *it*," Duffy said sourly.

O'Fallon said, "If they've bedded down, watchdogs'll be posted."

"Or maybe," York offered, "they're strung along the crick bank. Waiting for retaliation."

The former lawman shook his head, smirked skeptically. "What for? Not much chance of Bar-O boys or cattle trying to cross tonight. Don't know if any of the Bar-O outfit is even still breathing, but us."

York's shrug seemed easy, but it was calculated. "Might be down there celebrating. Big night for 'em, y'know. And I don't imagine Victoria Hammond invites the boys in for parties much."

O'Fallon's gaze remained steady. "You sound like you have something in mind, York."

"I do."

"Wal," Tulley said, "nothin' much brewin' in town. Might as well go somewheres and beat the boredom."

No one said anything. Tulley smiled at York. York

smiled back, though not as wide. The other two just looked at that money.

Finally O'Fallon said, "I'm game."

"Me too," Duffy said, and reached for the wad of cash.

But York plucked it away and pocketed it. "We'll settle up after. If they kill me, you know where to find it."

Duffy said, "What if *we* kill you?"

"What good," Tulley said, feeding shells into his shotgun, broken open over his arm, "is spendin' money when your head is blowed off?"

As they were saddling up, a figure in a satin gown moved through the moonlight up the boardwalk, hurriedly, and the worry on Rita Filley's face made it no less lovely.

She took York aside. "What are you preparing to do, Caleb?"

"What do you think?"

"Are you a lawman tonight, or some unholy avenger?"

"What would you have me be?"

She touched his face. "Alive when it's over."

Her kiss was sudden and brief but no less passionate.

Then she was gone, and shortly so was York and his small, expensive posse.

In a world washed ivory by moonlight, as stars kept silent vigil, York and his posse of three left their horses tied to scrawny trees among the spiny shrubs and bunch grass off the narrow lane to the Circle G. A short walk led to the fence-post archway to the handful of frame buildings and the single impressive structure among them, the one-story hacienda-like ranch house.

The sheriff led the way, handguns drawn and Tully

lugging his shotgun, moving into the compound, keeping low and slow. A slight breeze stirred brush and leaves, and a nocturnal songbird chimed in now and then. No sign presented itself of anyone standing guard among the structures, including the hacienda, where a window glowed with yellow lamplight. The bunkhouse with a cookhouse nearby was off to the right. No lights were on in either structure.

The four men headed that way.

Colt at the ready, York stepped to the door of the bunkhouse, a glorified shack much as the Bar-O's had been. He tried the door and found it unlocked. He opened it and went in fast, .44 moving right and then left, with the other three poised to follow him in and back him up.

The bunks were empty. The sitting area with potbellied stove was similarly unpopulated.

He closed the door, quietly.

Moving low and quick, he led his men to the left and the sheltering cottonwood. They were just tucking in back of its massive trunk when a guard revealed himself, coming around one side of the big adobe house.

They waited a few seconds. Then, peeking out, York snatched a look. The guard had positioned himself in front of the several steps to the porch; he was rolling a cigarette—a burly character with a cavalry shirt and a yellow bandanna knotted loose at his throat, his short-crowned hat bearing a telltale genuine rattlesnake band.

As the four huddled behind the broad cottonwood trunk, Duffy raised his left hand in a "hold on" motion, then with his right plucked a knife from a sheath on his left hip—the blade's blued finish gleaming in the moonlight. Duffy held the eight-inch throwing knife near the tip, exposing its leather-wrapped grip.

York gave him a look that said, *Are you sure?*

And Duffy gave him back a look that said, *Don't insult me.*

The watchdog, pleased with himself, was just lighting up a well-made cigarette when the blade thunked into the left side of his chest. He grunted, as if he'd been struck a blow with a fist. His legs gave away and he toppled hard on his back.

Duffy and O'Fallon scurried over and—after the tall knife thrower had retrieved his blade—dragged the dead man off, one on each arm, to some bushes on the far side of the cottonwood, where he'd not likely attract any attention.

Reporting back for duty, the two shootists paused as York raised a cautionary hand, and his expression told them to listen. From the direction of the creek came the echoey sound of rowdy carousing, muffled but distinct with raucous laughs occasionally rising above an overall murmuring clamor.

York smiled. He looked from face to face, and they knew the Circle G raiders were—as the sheriff had predicted—celebrating their victorious attack.

As they'd been instructed, Duffy and O'Fallon moved left and right, respectively, the former between the water tower and barn, the latter circling the cookhouse and bunkhouse. Duffy was heading upstream, O'Fallon down, with the idea being that York and Tulley would move through the towering trees beyond the hacienda. The sheriff and deputy would then position themselves at the edge of the stand of firs and York would fire the first shot.

There would be no callout for surrender, no "You're

under arrest." The raiders would get no more warning than the Bar-O bunkhouse got.

With .44 in hand, York sent the shotgun-toting Tulley to the left while he headed right, both into the pines, and it was a trickier journey than the other time he'd moved through the stand of firs as, despite the moonlight, the lack of sun shining down through high branches made getting through this forest of no paths truly a case of making your way in the dark. Add to that the need to make as little noise as possible, with the crushing of dry leaves and needles underfoot a dead (in several senses) giveaway, should any watcher be posted in these trees.

That smell of loam and grass and resin was the same, but the rest was some new nightmare he was slogging through. No animals were scurrying, but an owl wanted to know who the hell he was. The only thing keeping York from getting turned around and winding up back where he started or off to one side or the other was the echoing of drunken revelry bouncing off the nearby stream.

He was nearing the far edge of the fir stand when an arm looped around his neck and the flash of a blade not unlike the one that had killed that cigarette-rolling guard minutes ago came swiftly down seeking similar purchase when York brought his right elbow up, hard, and knocked into the wrist of his attacker and sent the knife flying God knew where in this darkness.

He thrust himself backward and the attacker, luckily, was forced back into a pine, with enough force to loosen that arm looped around his neck, which he slipped under, and in one swift motion he got the .44 out—*firing it would cause everything to go to hell, and would signal a general assault by his posse of three that it was not yet time to make*—and swung the weapon, landing it hard against the side of his attacker's head, to stun or even knock out that vague, threatening shape assailing him like a dream demon, just enough moonlight filtering through at that moment, at that angle, to reveal who his opponent was: *the Chiricahua Kid.*

The Kid was reeling from the blow, and without the knife that was an Apache's tool of close-in fighting, for a few moments York had the upper hand. He swung the .44 again, backhanded this time, and the second blow opened up a bloody gash from temple to cheek, then he head-butted the Indian, who was already pinned against the tree, and the Kid slid down the bark surface, gurgling.

York leaned down to hit him again, if need be, but the gurgling stopped and the man was dead or one hell of a faker. Moonlight found the knife and it glinted at York, as if to say, *Better safe than sorry.* York grabbed it up and pounded the blade into the fallen warrior's heart.

Dead for sure now.

York sat for a moment, the rough pinecone-strewn surface of the small forest making for uncomfortable seating; but he needed to catch his breath, leaning back against another fir. Enabled by night vision and a little moonlight, he regarded the dead renegade, and thought about what an ignoble end this storied fighter had come to. On the other hand, the son of a bitch had burned down that bunkhouse and caused the death of every man in it, so to hell with him.

He got to his feet and made his way to the edge of the trees. Positioned himself behind one, .44 nose pointed up.

And there they were.

The raiders laughing, slapping each other on the back, their glee echoing off ivory-glimmering waters gliding by, moving through the moon's reflection and leaving it behind on the northward journey. The sand looked like sugar, all right, whiter than sugar, as pure as these outlaw creatures cavorting on it were not.

The campfire at this end had four Circle G hands gathered around it, two sitting, two standing, passing a bottle around. A few others were sitting and standing between this point and the other campfire perhaps ten yards upstream. Across the way the white bank, glowing in ivory moonlight, looked pristine, unfouled by humanity.

Dave Carson, a onetime lawman himself, was strutting around, smoking a cigar, his close-set eyes giving him a dumber look than he maybe deserved.

York, behind a tree at the edge of the grassy incline down to the sand, leaned around and shot Carson in the head. It came apart like a melon and the cigar almost seemed to pause in midair before it dropped to the bank as men went for their guns and looked around them for cover, of which there was none. From the right came more gunfire—O'Fallon engaging the raiders—and, from upstream, Duffy's barrage began. Men wiggled and danced and died.

To the left a shotgun exploded from the trees—Tulley getting into the one-sided fray—and another Arizona Cowboy bought himself a ticket to the undertaker's display window, since the blast to the belly that killed him wouldn't show under the Sunday suit he'd be wearing to impress the mourners, if any.

A few of the rustlers turned cowboys went for their guns and returned fire, the reports echoing off the water, as if this were happening somewhere else and not right here.

The celebrants quickly died, thanks to whichever of the posse was closest by.

"*Hands in the air!*" York yelled. "*Or join your friends in hell!*"

All along the beach, the Circle G crew raised their arms and froze in place.

Between where York and Tulley were positioned, one man had brains enough to head into the trees, which after all provided the only cover—Billy Bassett, that skinny killer whose mustache overwhelmed his face, his Remington revolver firing at no one in particular, chewing up branches, as he slipped into the relative safety of the trees.

"*Round these prisoners up!*" York yelled to Tulley and the other two deputies, who converged as they herded captives.

The sheriff moved through the little forest as quickly as he could, hoping to get to the clearing that was the hacienda's backyard before Bassett did. He bumped into a tree, and another, and another, and it rocked him but didn't slow him much, though when he emerged he was reeling. He stood there getting his feet under him and looked around for Bassett.

Nowhere to be seen.

Had the outlaw's head start been enough for him to slip away entirely?

Then the little man with the big mustache emerged from the pines and planted himself for a moment, similarly needing to find his balance after his trip through those bewildering trees.

And the two men faced each other, perhaps four yards separating them, each breathing hard and with his six-gun hanging unholstered at his side.

Bassett looked at the sheriff with rage and disgust. "You . . . you're the killer they *say* you are, Caleb York."

"An expert opinion."

The hired gun's eyes were hard, his lips beneath the elaborate mustache soft and trembling. "You just . . . just up and shot Dave. *Killed* him. He never had a damn chance."

"Like the men in that bunkhouse. Anyway, Billy, I had a point to make."

"A point?"

"Only a handful died. In a fair fight, Sugar Creek would be running red."

"You're a *bastard*, York!"

The Remington came up.

The .44 came up faster.

"And you're a dead one," York said.

Billy's eyes looked up, as if checking to see if that really was a hole in his forehead. He was, of course, unable to confirm that, though the mist of red he left behind when his legs gave up and deposited him on his back on the grass did indeed affirm it, as did the gray-green soup of brains his head sank into, as if he were reclaiming them.

CHAPTER SIXTEEN

Aided by moonlight, Caleb York helped his deputies round up the seven survivors of the shoot-out at Sugar Creek, disarming them, herding them into a hands-up group near the Circle G's horse barn behind which the water tower loomed.

Rope was cut in strips, each captive made to get on horseback and have his wrists bound to the saddle horn, as the little posse prepared to convey the prisoners back to Trinidad.

Tulley looked unhappy.

York asked him why.

"Where's Jonathan P. Tulley gonna sleep tonight?" he pondered aloud.

With a nod toward the prisoners on horseback, York said, "Sit up with them till I can spell you, then you can borrow my hotel room."

Tulley beamed. "The good Lord broke the mold makin' ye, Caleb York."

"Didn't he, though."

The bookkeeper, Byers, in the derby and cutaway jacket he'd worn when York first encountered him, hustled out of the ranch house with a carpetbag in hand. He waddled up to York, who was supervising, and said, "Two things, Sheriff."

"Which are?"

"The mistress requests an audience in the library."

"When I get around to it."

The bookkeeper's head tilted sideways. "And I was wondering . . . might I collect my personal steed and make my way elsewhere?"

York grinned, laughed once. "Be my guest, Mr. Byers."

The gray-mustached former factotum tipped his derby and was heading into the horse barn when York said, "And Mr. Byers?"

The stout little fellow turned to face the sheriff. "Yes, sir?"

"Perhaps you might be more prudent in selecting your next employer."

"Excellent advice, sir." He gave a little bow. "And good evening. Or is it morning now?"

"Not really keeping track. Might I suggest the Trinidad House for the night, rather than setting out for parts unknown at such an hour?"

"More first-rate advice."

And Byers slipped into the barn.

Fifteen minutes or so later, York saw the little three-deputy-and-seven-prisoner caravan off and then the sheriff was alone in the Circle G compound.

Only the rush of water filtering back through the pines remained to keep him company, the songbirds apparently out of tunes to share, small creatures and their predators alike sleeping between encounters, the breeze dying down enough to leave leaves and brush alone. Even the bookkeeper was gone. No sign of the pretty little serving girl, either. Perhaps she slept. Perhaps she'd slipped away less openly than Byers.

At any rate, when York entered the house, the emptiness was emphasized by a darkness only mildly alleviated by the moon creeping in windows. Still, he had no problem making his way to the library, where he opened the heavy door to find Victoria Hammond pacing slowly on the chamber's midroom Oriental carpet. She halted, hearing him come in, her eyes going to him, where he stood framed in the doorway.

The woman was always a rather remarkable sight for a man's eyes to take in and his mind to assess. But tonight Victoria Hammond made a picture so striking he would never forget it.

All that ebony hair was down and bouncing on her shoulders, nothing pinned up or back, giving her a look as wild as any animal. She had applied face paint as bold as any bordello wench's, yet she looked beautiful and somehow not at all cheap. Her clothing was such that he'd never seen a woman wearing anything like it, not even on a theater stage—a black silk shirt under a black leather vest, black gaucho trousers, pointed-toe boots with heels so high she would easily reach his eyes.

And on her right hip, worn as low as any man-killer's, was an elaborately tooled holster, tan against the black apparel, with a pearl-gripped Colt .45 revolver, perfectly positioned for her slender fingers to touch the handle, if her arm hung loose and natural.

Which it did.

"Caleb," she said.

"Mrs. Hammond."

He stepped in, shut the door behind him.

She gestured toward the love seat. "Shall we sit?"

"I think not."

The would-be cattle baroness turned sideways, folded

her arms, looking away from him. The sitting area, over-seen by her husband's standing portrait, was at her back.

She said, "I lost another son tonight."

"Condolences," he said.

Still not looking at him, she asked, flatly, "Do you in-tend to arrest me?"

"I do." York strolled over, got in front of and faced her, the desk at his back, the woman maybe six feet from him, her husband staring over her shoulder. "You shot Willa Cullen."

Her chin came up. Her eyes were steady and half-lidded. ". . . I did. That woman killed my son Pierce. It's a mother's right, settling such a score. A lioness would do the same."

He raised an eyebrow. "I killed your William. Were you settling up for that when you sent Clay Colman to kill me at the graveyard? And to ambush me at night in town?"

She shook her head and all that dark hair came along for the ride. "That was Colman's own doing. I knew nothing of it, any of it. He had a personal grudge, I hear."

"You heard right."

A shrug. The dark eyes remained steady. "I instructed my ramrod to work *with* you. I was unaware of the ac-tions he took on his own. I *told* him you were on our side of this." Another shrug. "At the time, I thought you were."

York frowned. "*Your* side? The law's side. I'm a peace officer, woman."

With a regal smile, she said, "You didn't sow much peace tonight, did you, Sheriff?"

He huffed a laugh. "Did you give me much choice? As for you impulsively trying to settle up with Willa, you may be relieved to hear she may recover."

Her eyelashes fluttered just a bit, as she digested this news. "Uh, well. That's a relief to learn. Of course."

"So I heard from her lips that you shot her. Which confirms that you knew about the raid on the Bar-O. That you sent those attackers in to burn and murder."

Her chin came up. "I did no such thing. I knew nothing of it! The first I became aware of what they'd done was when they reported my son's murder."

"His murder?"

Indignation now. "What would *you* call it?"

"Self-defense. The ranch was attacked and Willa stood her ground. That's what we do in the Southwest." He laughed harshly. "You expect me to believe you didn't orchestrate that raid? After you returned yourself to launch a second assault?"

Now the dark arching eyebrows rose. "Can you prove I dispatched those men? They quite naturally developed an animosity against a rival team of gunmen. And my son, Pierce . . ." She stopped, swallowed. ". . . Pierce is the one who organized what you call a raid, or so it would seem. He must have wanted to impress his mother, the poor misguided soul."

Her chin trembled, whether out of emotion or at her bidding for effect, he couldn't guess.

She added, "He should have known that wasn't necessary to win . . . win his mother's love."

She swallowed; tears were pooling.

York's smile settled on one side of his face. "Mrs. Hammond, you are a rare woman indeed. Willing to sell out your own dead son, just hours after his passing, to cover your misdeeds. I've seen a lot in my day, lady, but never anything like this. Anything like *you*."

She came to him, slowly, no sudden moves, cutting the distance in half. "I hope the Cullen girl lives. What I did was rash . . . wrong. But I think any judge, any jury, would understand a mother's anguished, misguided act."

"I thought Pierce was the misguided one."

"Caleb, Caleb . . . if the Cullen girl does live," she insisted, her expression softening, "she will return to a life much changed. Buildings burned down, cattle wasting away, her people dead . . . she'll be so alone. Dejected and dismayed, her hopes, her dreams dashed."

"A reasonable assumption."

She moved even closer. "I can make it up to her, for what I did to her tonight, so . . . so impetuously. That offer of mine, that insulting offer I made for her holdings? I'll replace it with one commensurate with the property's actual value."

He shook his head slowly, his smile openly bitter. "Everything that's happened tonight, and you can think of business?"

She looked to the sky—or the ceiling, anyway. "What am I left with *but* business *to* consider? I have one remaining son—Hugh—who is himself a brilliant man of commerce . . . but he has turned away from me. If I can make the Circle G a going concern, an attractive prospect . . . and with his brothers both gone? That heart of his grown so cold may yet warm to his mother. I *can* bring him back into the fold. Bring him back into my loving grasp."

Grasp is the right word, he thought.

"All you have to do," York said, "is convince the woman you tried to kill tonight that doing business with you is a golden opportunity."

She smiled; it tightened her eyes, and the redness of the face paint screamed at him even as her voice was soft as silk, and as slick.

"*You're* the one who can do that, Caleb. If you can

convince Willa Cullen to sell me the Bar-O, at a price that's better than fair . . . after all, her cattle are dying of thirst and her ranch buildings are mostly burned out, so it's really just the land that has any value . . ."

York glared at her. "Her property is devalued because you burned it out! Her cattle are dying because you denied the animals water, and her people are gone because your men killed them. Interesting damn way to bring the market value down, lady."

She ignored that; her left hand gripped his right arm. Her throaty voice grew soft, seductive.

"If you can convince her, Caleb, I will make you a full partner. You don't have to invest a dime. You won't have to be part of a single thing to do with the business. I know you have no inclination toward being a cattleman—it's not what you do, or who you are. So you stay sheriff and marshal and police chief and whatever badge they push your way—you can earn your keep by helping me make sure Trinidad and San Miguel County throw no obstacles in my path . . . in *our* path."

The tips of their noses almost brushed now.

"Do you know how many men died tonight, woman?"

"No. Do you?" She slipped an arm around his waist, drew her body to his. "I told you before, Caleb. I can use a strong man. And I still have a few child-bearing years left. Perhaps you can give me another son."

Damn her! She still smelled of lilacs.

Through his teeth he said, "A son to replace the one I took away from you? Or maybe the one you sent to his death tonight?"

She pushed him away, hard, her expression suddenly savage. Taking several steps back, her upper lip curling back over her teeth, she said, "Arrest me, then. Take me to a judge and see how I fare."

"You're facing a judge right now."

Victoria Hammond shook her head in slow disbelief. "You're a lawman, Caleb. You're not some gun for hire, like the rabble who died on both sides tonight." Very casually, she added, "And you're certainly not a man who would kill a woman—are you?"

"Might be."

She went for her gun, the lovely face clenched into sheer ugliness and utter evil now, but York drew so quick his bullet entered her and exited before she even had the weapon out of its fancy holster, the thunder of the .44's report shaking things in the room.

York grunted. "Seems I am."

She looked down at the red-rimmed hole in her belly and a trickle of red trailed down, shimmering over the black silk. Then she crumpled to the floor, a curtain that slipped off its rod, and began weeping like a little girl—likely with gut-shot pain and utter disappointment and maybe at an outcome she could not talk or scheme her way clear of.

But surely not regret.

And her dead husband looked down from his gilt-edged frame with no sympathy at all.

CHAPTER SEVENTEEN

When Caleb York rode into town, going on midnight, he noted the light in Doc Miller's office window. He quickly hopped down, tied the gelding up at the hitching post in front of the bank, and hurried up the exterior stairs hugging the building. That he was exhausted made no difference at all.

As York entered, the doctor was coming into the waiting area from his surgery with a cup of coffee he'd prescribed himself. His living quarters were beyond that, including a spare bedroom used for patients needing particular care.

"Caleb," the plump little man said pleasantly, as if this were a social call. He looked rumpled but pleased with himself.

"How is she?" York asked with urgency bursting, as he hung his coat and hat on the tree by the door.

The physician plopped himself down at the chair behind his cluttered desk. "Alive. Fever broke, and never got past one hundred degrees. Good signs."

Looming from the wall in back of Dr. Albert Miller were framed diplomas hanging askew, as if they too had a hard night. The skeleton the doc called Hippocrates seemed to be listening intently from his corner as York stood before Miller, leaning in, a hand on the desktop.

"I'll keep her here for a few days at least," the doctor was saying. "If you can spare Tulley, I'll put him on bedpan duty and he can haul food in from the café. Just soup at first."

York sighed with relief, closed his eyes for a moment, then drew up a chair and sat, still facing the physician intently. "You'd say she's doing well, then?"

Doc nodded. Sipped his coffee. "The bullet went in and out, so I didn't have to go digging. I guess I don't have to tell you that shreds of cloth getting into a wound like hers can kill you deader than any bullet. But that silk camisole she was wearing was a godsend. Didn't tear the way that cotton shirt of hers did. Much cleaner puncture."

"Can I see her?"

Miller yawned. "Well, she's awake, and I've just given her a dose of laudanum that'll put her out before you know it. But go on in, Caleb. Do her good to see your ugly face."

York moved quickly into the doctor's apartment and through to the sick room off at left, a glorified cubbyhole with a dresser and a metal bed and little else. Her head on a plump feather pillow, her hair still braided up, Willa was in a white hospital-type gown, her face bloodless but beautiful, her pale Nordic features taking on a new fragility.

The lamp on a corner table was turned low, but it— and moonlight from the window to her right as she lay there—made his presence known to her. A smile traced her lips as he drew up a chair next to her bedside and sat.

"Caleb . . . Caleb . . ."

"Shush, now. You just be quiet, woman. Doc Miller says you're going to be fine."

Her smooth forehead frowned a little, probably as much as she could manage. "What's to become of me, Caleb? What's to become of us?"

"We'll decide that. Raymond Parker's going to help out, and I'll work hand in hand with him. We'll make sure that beef of yours gets rightly watered. Don't you worry none."

"The ranch house is standing," she said, brow smooth again. "I can rebuild the rest." Her eyes welled. "But so many were . . . were *slaughtered.* . . ."

He took a hand of hers and held it with both of his. "Don't you think about that now. Just know this. A whole new future lies ahead for us."

Her eyebrows managed to lift. "Here in town? Or at the . . . the Bar-O?"

He gave her a gentle smile. "At one of them. We'll decide together."

Her eyes widened and she tried to sit up, but the pain—laudanum or not—stopped her. Half rising, York gently settled her back into the pillow.

"Caleb," she said. Softer. Barely audible.

He leaned in.

She said weakly, but distinct: "What about . . . about that woman? The Hammond woman?"

"Dead."

"Dead . . . ?"

"I killed her."

She beamed, obviously in a narcotic haze. "Oh, Caleb! That's . . . that's the sweetest thing you ever did for me."

He kissed the tip of her nose.

"We aim to please," he said.

A TIP OF
THE STETSON

In following the late Mickey Spillane's lead—established in his various film script drafts and notes about the York character and his world—I have been more concerned with the mythic West than the real one.

The first in the series, *The Legend of Caleb York* (2015), based on Mickey's unproduced screenplay, clearly takes an approach in the Hollywood tradition. This appeals to me, as I grew up on John Wayne, Randolph Scott, Joel McCrea, and Audie Murphy movies, as well as American television's Western craze of the late fifties, *Maverick* my personal favorite.

But I hope to present the mythic West in a framework of the real one, providing authentic underpinnings to my fanciful tales, much as a *noir* detective novel sets melodrama against a gritty reality. So I am of course indebted to research, and while I no doubt have overlooked some sources, I should at least acknowledge the ones that were particularly helpful.

I would guess that most (if not all) of my contemporaries in the Western fiction field use the following two sources: *Everyday Life in the Wild West from 1840–1900* (1999), Candy Moulton; and *The Writer's Guide to*

Everyday Life in the 1800s (1993), Marc McCutcheon. Of the numerous books on firearms in my library, I lean upon *Guns of the American West* (2009), Dennis Adler. Previous novels in this series all drew upon these invaluable sources.

For this novel, depicting the aftermath of the Blizzard of 1886–1887 (the central concern of the previous Caleb York novel, *Hot Lead, Cold Justice*), I again consulted *Cattle Kingdom: The Hidden History of the Cowboy West* (2017), Christopher Knowlton; and *The Real Wild West: The 101 Ranch and the Creation of the American West* (1999), Michael Wallis; as well as the more recently published article "The Big Die-Up," Chuck Lyons, *Wild West* magazine, April 2019. Sources new to this novel include *Happy Trails: A Dictionary of Western Expressions* (1994), Robert Hendrickson; and *Famous Sheriffs and Western Outlaws* (1929), William MacLeod Raine.

I really don't know how I managed to write historical novels prior to Internet search engines, when I had to depend on such old-fashioned methods as newspaper, magazine, and book research. Now—as I imagine is the case for most writers of fiction working today setting their stories yesterday—I do a lot of it as I go, utilizing Google.

Web addresses are not included, as those change and disappear from time to time, but I will provide selected article names and authors (and sometimes Web sites).

Helpful in my depiction of a real-life Las Vegas, New Mexico, crime boss, was "Vicente Silva—Leading Silva's White Caps Gang," Kathy Weiser-Alexander (at the excellent *Legends of America* site); "Hiding in Plain Sight—Frontier Crime Lord," Tom Rizzo (at his Web site); and "Crime Boss Vicente Silva," Mark Boardman, *True West*. That magazine's column "Ask the Marshall" by Marshall Trimble has been helpful in a more general manner.

Also useful was "Las Vegas, New Mexico—As Wicked as Dodge City," Kathy Weiser (again at the *Legends of America* site); and "Getting Lost in History in the Other Las Vegas," Steven Talbot, *New York Times*.

I also wish to acknowledge the Western Fictioneers, an organization founded by Robert J. Randisi, James Reasoner, Frank Roderus, and other professional writers of Western novels and short stories (I'm a member). Their discussion group was extremely valuable to me here, on several occasions fielding research questions I couldn't answer in my source books or on the Net. Thanks in particular go to Vicky Rose and Gordon Rottman.

Also, thank you to my supportive editor, Michaela Hamilton; my agent and friend, Dominick Abel; and my wife (and in-house editor), Barbara Collins.